Capturing Karma

The Sullivan Boys, Book Three

by

K. M. Daughters

Capturing Karma

Cover Art by *Kim Mendoza*

The Wild Rose Press
PO Box 708
Adams Basin, NY 14410-0706
Visit us at www.thewildrosepress.com

Publishing History
First Crimson Rose Edition, 2010
Print *ISBN:* 1-60154-721-8

Published in the United States of America

"Hi, Brian," she responded, tamping down the temptation to hug him hello. "How's the new baby doing?"

"Great, thanks. How's that bump on your head?"

Matilda touched an edge of one of the butterfly strips over her eyebrow. "Turning every color of the rainbow, but it's fine."

He swiveled his head toward the throaty bark of the wolfhound in the corner of the room, then scanned the other occupants in the lounge: primate, feline, porcine, wolfish and human. "Steve told me you're a great vet. Looks like you're pretty swamped here."

"Shamus and I split the patient load," she said.

"And Shamus is?"

"My brother. He came for me at the hospital yesterday?"

Brian's eyes bored into her, a sexy smile twitched the corner of his lips. "Good."

"And 'good' means?"

"The big guy isn't competition. That's good."

"Ah. So we're clear. What competition would that be?"

The sexy smile twitched again. "For but a smile from sweet Matty," he lilted in an Irish brogue.

Squelching an impulse to grin, she molded her face serious and parroted a brogue, "Ah but woe to the knave who plies smiles with an untrue heart."

She grinned now. "What can I do for you, Brian? Did you get an estimate to repair your car?"

"It's about that letter you brought me. It's related to a case. We need your help."

Of course. "I gave you the letter. You know as much as I do." Her heart hammered, nothing to do with the pulse acceleration from earlier flirtation. *I can't go further with this case. No matter what, I have to stay anonymous.*

Dedication

For Tom, Jen, Mike, Kate, Brian, Emilie, Jeff, Natalie and Michael John. You are our hearts.

Acknowledgements

Our editor, Joelle Walker, inspires our respect,
admiration and deep appreciation. Joelle is our
champion, our cheerleader and our treasured friend.
Thank you, Joelle, for taking us with you.
Thank you, also, to Dr. Kirsten and Dr. Jeff Zeitler
for consulting with us. We really appreciate your
sharing your pharmaceutical knowledge with us.
And we are blessed to know you.

Praise for K.M. Daughters

Book One: AGAINST DOCTORS ORDERS
"Daughters has crafted an intriguing story, full of detailed scenes and fascinating, believable characters. Crisp dialogue and an even balance of action and drama keep the pages turning. If men enjoy mystery as much as women love romance, then Daughters may have created the best of both worlds. The only problem could arise when it comes to deciding who reads the next Sullivan Boys novel first...him or her. I highly recommend [this one] and I look forward to the sequels. 5 Stars."
~W. R. Potter, Reader's Choice Literary Reviews
"Watch out...the Sullivan Boys are a force to be reckoned with! *AGAINST DOCTORS ORDERS* packs a punch and keeps you turning the pages."
~Brenda Novak, NY Times Bestselling Author

Book Two, BEYOND THE CODE OF CONDUCT
"This compelling novel has a liberal amount of sexual tension, interesting characters and covert ops. But Bobbie and Joe's real challenge begins when their undercover assignment is over."
~Donna M. Brown, RT Book Reviews
"Ms. Daughters has done it again with a classic romantic suspense read! This story is hot hot hot!...I couldn't have asked for a better read."
~Val Pearson, You Gotta Read Book Reviews
"An engrossing and hard to put down story!"
~A. Pohren, Café of Dreams Book Reviews
"Romantic suspense just doesn't get any better than this!...I couldn't put the book down. I read it cover to cover in one night...*BEYOND THE CODE OF CONDUCT* is romantic, it's filled with suspense, and it's one book that I would love to read again."

Happy birthday, dear Mother. Yes, I'm singing this. Only for you, Mom. Only for you.

You think I forgot. Or maybe you know I remember, but want you to think I forgot. Spiteful little brat, you're probably thinking. Can't blame you, really. The things I said to you before I left—all that flush and steam of arguing must have hurt like hell. You probably watched my back when I wouldn't turn around and wave goodbye. Pretty thoughtless of me. Stupid, actually, considering what's happened since.

I don't regret my decision to leave, though. It was a pretty good ride. Can't beat the rush from pushing the Harley hard for a couple of hours. Plenty of willing tail waiting for me downstate, too. Amazing how quickly I shacked up and spread out. Always had a way with the ladies. Even you couldn't stay mad at me for long. Are you mad at me now, Mother? Yeah, probably, because you think I forgot your birthday.

Well, I haven't forgotten—your birthday or anything else. I remember every word you flashed at me—every do this and don't do that. Repercussions, Jake, you have to consider the repercussions. You are the company you keep—blah, blah, blah. I suppose it takes a man to admit that he was wrong. OK, so I'm a man now, Mother. I was wrong. And you were right. If you could hear me, you'd be nodding and smiling that knowing smile. I don't want to hurt you more than I already have, but you don't know everything, either.

It doesn't matter anymore. Hear me now, Mom.

Please hear me. Ironic, I managed to hide from you, but now all I want to be is found. Find me, Mom. Secret code—Kachoom Bombay.

Please find me.

Chapter 1

Brian Sullivan caught the brown blur in motion aimed straight for him out of the corner of his eye. He gripped the wheel and gave the engine some juice to slip through the intersection, out of the oncoming car's path. *It's not going to hit me.*

The jolt of impact and grind of metal scraping metal proved him wrong. Slamming on the brakes, he jerked the wheel hard right to get the jeep to the curb and rammed the gearshift into park.

After smashing into Brian's jeep the compact car ricocheted off and continued on a path of destruction, skinning layers of paint off two parked cars on the opposite side of the street before a tree stopped its progress.

"No! No! No!" Brian slapped his hand on the steering wheel. Already late, he did *not* need this today. *Joe is going to kill me.*

Instinctively he shoved out the door and stomped across the street to check on the driver. He wrestled with the temptation to call the desk to report the accident and have one of his buddies roll on this one. Then he could make it to the church before his family had his head. But he couldn't. As a police officer it was his duty to serve, even if his duty as his brother's best man at the imminent wedding demanded top priority.

Brian neared the car. Not too bad, damage-wise, considering—a smashed right fender panel, probably lost strips of paint on the left side judging from the angry gouges in the parked cars lined behind it and the front bumper was toast. The woman slumped over the steering wheel inside the car prompted him to sprint the rest of the way.

Yanking the driver's door open, he leaned over her. "Miss, you all right?"

She lifted her head slowly and stared at him, eyes glazed.

The clouds in those chocolate eyes heightened their haunting, mesmerizing affect on Brian. He hadn't forgotten Matilda Connors' hypnotic eyes, had seen them in dreams since she had visited his squad room and delivered a message from his dead brother.

A nasty gash over her eye oozed some blood. Brian snatched a handkerchief out of his tuxedo pocket and pressed it on the cut. "Matilda? Do you need medical assistance?"

"You let your hair grow." A smile twitched on her lips. "I was right. It does soften your face."

"What?" The handkerchief dampened beneath his fingers. He gently removed it, refolded and clamped it harder against her forehead.

"Ow." Her hand shot up and grabbed his.

Tingles traveled up his arm, warming, shocking, the identical sensations he had experienced the last time she touched him—lost and found at the same time.

He drew back, bowed under the car's doorframe. "Sorry. Your head's bleeding."

"I'm sorry. This is all my fault. I didn't even see your car in the intersection. You were the only one that came to mind after I wrote the letter down. I was rushing out to give it you."

"A letter?" Brian still reeled from the aftereffect of the brief electricity-like contact with her hand. "From Jimmy?"

Her huge eyes were vacant.

Brian connected the dots for her. "My brother. The Susan Anderson lead you gave me after Jimmy pointed you toward me? Thank you, by the way."

"Oh right. No, this is a letter from Jake."

Her hand drifted up to the wound, dotting her

fingers crimson. Brian opened the handkerchief, swabbed her hand with the maroon-spotted cloth and scrunched it in a messy knot against her head. She swatted his arm.

"Leave it for a minute," he commanded. "Who's Jake?"

"I don't know his last name. I copied the letter down word for word."

"He dictated it? What did he look like?"

"No, I didn't see him. I saw the letter."

"I don't get it. Where?"

"In my head."

Here we go again. Off balance, Brian assessed her. Too pale and probably delirious. *Better call for an ambulance.*

"OK. Give me the letter," he conceded. "I'll take care of it."

He accepted the crumbled paper she picked off the passenger seat and jammed it in his jacket pocket.

"Can you move your car or do you want me to do it? Do I need to call a tow truck?"

Silent, she looked intently at him and lifted a shaky hand to her brow again, partially dislodging the makeshift bandage, smearing their intertwined fingers with blood.

"I'm calling an ambulance." He let her hold the handkerchief and dug in his pocket for his phone.

"The hospital," she replied.

"No problem."

"Not me. You need to go the hospital."

"Me? No, I'm fine."

"Yes, you need to go to the hospital instead of the church."

"I don't need...did you say church?"

"Yes. Joe and Bobbie are already at the hospital."

"How do you know that?" Shaking his head, he remembered a similar, spooky exchange between

5

them. "Don't answer that. Do you know if they are OK?"

"The baby is coming."

Brian wasted no time questioning how Matilda knew about the baby or Bobbie. "Sit back for a minute." Stretching over her, he twisted the ignition key, immersed in the citrus scent of her perfume and the faint, metallic scent of her blood.

When her car wouldn't start he stood up, called the desk and ordered a tow truck. "The car is on Elm, just past the Main Street intersection. Wrong side of the road against a tree. Can't miss it. I'm heading to the hospital with the driver. She has a head gash and Joe's about to be a father. Yeah, thanks, Nagle, I'll tell him."

"I don't need to go to the hospital," Matilda protested as he pocketed the phone.

"I think you might need a stitch or two. That cut looks deep. Don't argue. Let's just go…please."

Solemnly, she accepted his outstretched hand and he hoisted her out of the car. Her legs wobbled, so Brian put his arm around her and half-carried her to the jeep.

She eased into the passenger seat and Brian rounded the rear of the car. He dealt a swift kick to the dangling rear bumper and knocked it more or less back where it belonged.

Speeding toward the hospital, logic intervened. *What the hell am I doing taking her word that Bobbie's in labor? I should have called Joe before I detoured away from the church.*

Calculating time lost once at the ambulance bay of the hospital, Brian helped Matilda out of the car. *At least she'll get attention for the cut on her head and I can race to the church and beg Joe's forgiveness if Bobbie isn't here.*

Inquiring at the desk, Brian confirmed Roberta Leighton had been admitted as a maternity patient. The receptionist directed Brian and Matilda to the second floor of the hospital.

****

Matilda caught the bouquet of roses that flew out the door toward her midriff.

Brian laughed. "Nice catch. I think we have the right room." He braced her shoulders with cupped hands and nudged her into the maternity suite ahead of him.

Matilda's eyes widened at the dizzying scene. Strikingly handsome men in black tie towered above tuxedo-clad, little-boy miniatures who played tag, whooped and ran circles around each other and grown-ups' legs. A lovely, fair-haired, petite woman dressed in a flowing, sea-foam, strapless gown rattled non-stop admonitions to the screaming kids, the noise deafening. Two pretty teenaged girls wearing spaghetti-strapped, cocktail-length versions of the woman's gown, shepherded identical twin girls. The kids twirled in nausea-inducing spins, frothy petticoats flying beneath mint-colored party dresses. A row of varying-sized bridal bouquets lined the wide windowsill.

"Welcome to the crazy world of the Sullivan's," Brian remarked, wrapping an arm around her shoulder and pushing her into the fray. "Don't worry. They don't bite."

Matilda set the bouquet of roses down on the sill and surveyed the room.

The woman on the hospital bed, around whom the well-dressed circus milled, and next to whom a quite gorgeous man wearing a black, silk eye patch hovered, boomed, "I wouldn't marry you, Sullivan, if you were the last man on the planet. I hate you. Don't touch me. Ow. Ow. Ow!"

Matilda raised an eyebrow in Brian's direction. "The bride and groom?"

He leaned down and whispered in her ear, "That's my delicate, future sister-in-law, Bobbie and the guy with the eye patch hanging over her bed is my brother, Joe."

"You will marry me this minute, Roberta. Tell her, Ma." Joe lasered a sapphire eye at a demure woman with identical eye color and a gleaming cap of snowy hair clad in an emerald, satin, floor-length gown. The apparent matriarch of the family astutely kept her lips pressed together.

Joe turned back toward his laboring bride. "My son will have my name, Bobbie. Don't you dare have this baby yet."

"My daughter will be a Leighton, you..." Bobbie fell back in the bed panting, a contraction forestalling her retaliating salvo. A mane of auburn curls fanned on the pillow, mascara smudges beneath her eyes.

The men in the room gazed anywhere but at the bed.

Dazed, Matilda took a deep breath.

"Hey, Brian. Have to hit girls over the head to date you, huh?" A huge man, maybe as tall as Matilda's brother, around six foot six, with close-cropped, strawberry blond hair and gleaming, blue eyes sauntered toward her. "Hi, I'm Patrick Sullivan."

Matilda shook his extended hand, smiling. "Hi, I'm Matilda. Actually, I hit Brian, not the other way around."

"Right," Brian added. "Matilda isn't my date. We had a fender bender. I want Molly to check out that cut on her head. Geez, it's swelling, but at least the bleeding stopped."

Matilda brushed her hand over the tender wound and winced.

"Where's Molly?" Brian asked the room.

A blonde pixie in a white lab jacket over the seemingly requisite sea-foam dress marched briskly into the room. "Did I hear my name?"

Matilda spun within Brian's encompassing hold

on her shoulder toward the woman.

"Hi Mol. Can you look at Matilda's head?" Brian requested.

"She's with Brian. So I'm sure there's something wrong with her head," a long-legged man razzed from the side of the room. He unfolded from his position leaning against the radiator, crossed the room and kissed Molly on the lips.

"Nice, Dan, real nice. My brother, Danny," Brian announced shaking his head.

"Nice to meet you, Danny." Matilda shook his hand, twice the size of her own.

"Matilda, look at me," Molly demanded.

A white-haired gentleman, whom Matilda assumed was Brian's dad, jumped from his seat and offered it to her. She gratefully accepted and sat down, exhausted by the Sullivan clan.

Matilda stared into Molly's keen, probing eyes and followed Molly's instruction to track a penlight she flashed back and forth.

"Any dizziness or nausea?" Molly asked, sliding the penlight in her pocket.

"A little shaky getting out of the car, but no, I'm fine."

"Good. How did this happen?"

"I must have split it open against the steering wheel." Matilda glanced around the room.

"Pretty overwhelming, aren't they?" Molly probed the cut over Matilda's eye with cool fingers. "It's superficial, but since it's on your face, we'll stitch it so it heals properly. I'll page someone up here to help you."

"This isn't working!" Bobbie hollered.

All eyes focused on the bed.

"I can't do this, Molly." Bobbie moaned, pitched and arched her back in the grip of another contraction. "I changed my mind."

"You *can* do this, honey." Molly scurried bedside and held Bobbie's hand. "All of you, out," Molly ordered. She stared over Bobbie's stomach at Joe. "You stay."

The excused Sullivan men obviously couldn't get out of there fast enough. The elegant woman sitting next to Matilda rose as Danny, Patrick, their father and a slim, teenaged boy left the room.

"Amy and Mary, take the little ones out with your uncles and stay together in the waiting room. Father Don, do something. I don't care what you say, but marry these two and make it legal," the refined woman said, her soft voice at odds with her drill sergeant's orders.

"Jean, you know I can't outside of church," a man in gray slacks and a black, turtleneck sweater replied.

"Yes, you can and you will. I promise you I will have them in your church as soon as possible, but until then, do whatever it takes."

Matilda widened her eyes when the priest nodded. *This lady could probably get God to follow her orders.*

"Brian stay where you are." Mrs. Sullivan's tone, albeit low volume, carried a take-no-prisoners inflexion. "You're the best man. Where are the rings? By the way..." She clasped Matilda's hand. "I'm Jean Sullivan, the mother and grandmother of this unruly brood."

"Pleasure to meet you at this interesting occasion." Matilda grinned.

Jean rolled her eyes and chuckled.

"This isn't official, Jean. You understand?" The priest tilted his head and gazed at Jean evenly.

"Official enough for the moment." Jean's soft voice somehow rang with command.

The remaining family clustered around the bed in the labor room while the priest recited the vows for Joe and Bobbie to repeat, pausing twice when Molly coached Bobbie through the peaks and valleys of contractions.

"I now pronounce you husband and wife," Father Don concluded.

"The baby is coming. I want to push, Molly." Bobbie clutched Molly's forearm, eyes huge. "Can I push now?"

Brian caught Matilda's eye and jerked his head in the direction of the door. She jumped up and followed him into the hallway.

"Wow." Brian wiped sweat from his forehead.

Matilda giggled. "Yep, that was a 'wow' situation."

"I'm sorry for dragging you into the middle of that insanity."

"Oh, don't apologize. Maybe I'm insane, too. I enjoyed meeting your family. Are they always so noisy?"

"No. They're usually louder."

"OK, double-wow."

Brian laughed and swung an arm around her shoulder, heightening Matilda's sense of belonging with him and his family. "There are so many of you."

"And one was AWOL. Everyone was in there except my brother-in-law, Mike. He must be around here somewhere. He's a surgeon at this hospital. Let's find a place to sit down."

Leading Matilda to a couch in the waiting area, Brian sat beside her. The men clustered around the television, rapt attention on a college football game. The kids paid fleeting attention to a read-aloud story from either Amy or Mary—no one had yet paired the teenage girls to names for Matilda.

"Does your mother always boss priests around?" Matilda gazed at Brian, excited by his nearness, the radiant warmth from his body that cosseted her, his clean, soapy smell. Far from the official mission that had her racing into her car and bashing into him earlier, but more than pleasant to sit by his side.

"Father Don is family. He and my parents were classmates and have been friends since grade school.

But, don't mess with Jean Sullivan. She keeps us boys in check without ever raising her voice. In fact, when her voice gets softer, we know we're really in trouble."

Joe Sullivan raced into the lounge, arms upraised in victory. "It's a girl. Emma Jean Sullivan."

The family hooted, whistled, clapped and hollered, patted backs and hugged each other. They toned it down when a nurse appeared and reminded them they were in a hospital.

Matilda was included in the hug fest, Brian last to take his turn with her. He scooped her off her feet and swung her around. She froze as their lips met, melded, soft, a hint of peppermint on his breath. Every nerve ending ignited as he lingered in the kiss and suspended her in a far loftier place than a few inches off the ground.

Brian ended the delicious, dizzying connection abruptly. "Sorry. I was caught up in the moment."

Set back on her feet with a jarring thud, "Uh—no problem. Me, too." *Can't say I'm sorry except that it didn't last longer.*

"Bri, come on." Joe tugged Brian's arm. "Molly said only two at a time could come in and see my daughter. You're my best man, so you're first."

"Want to see the baby?" Brian asked.

"Try and stop me," Matilda declared.

Bobbie lay on the pillow, her copper-colored hair framing her face like a rosy halo. She cradled a tiny, pink-swaddled bundle in her arms. Joe smiled and made way for them bedside, leaning against the doorframe, arms folded.

Matilda bent near, Brian beside her. "Ooh, she is beautiful," she cooed at the baby, so like the mother who held her. The infant's red hair curled around her porcelain face, her tiny mouth a pink bud.

"She's downright gorgeous. Just like you, sis."

Brian kissed the crown of Emma's head.

"Thank you." Bobbie beamed at them. "Sorry I was so crazy before."

"A wild woman." Brian planted a kiss on Bobbie's cheek.

"No problem. How many women get married while in the throes of labor? I'm Matilda. Slammed my car into your brother-in-law a while ago." The baby curled tiny fingers around Matilda's outstretched hand, Emma's impossibly miniscule fingernails pearly half moons.

"We've got to get that cut tended to," Brian said.

"Matilda?" Bobbie scrutinized her face. "Are you the lady who talked to Jimmy about Susan Anderson?"

"Yes, I am."

"I owe you a big thank you. Your information helped us solve the case."

"I'm glad."

Patrick poked his head through the door.

"When can we meet our niece?"

"In a minute." Joe shoved Patrick's head back out the door, refolded his arms over his middle and smiled at them.

"Brian, you have to bring Matilda over one night," Bobbie suggested. "I would love to talk to you about your gift." She shifted the tiny baby in her arms.

"Will do." Leaning forward, Brian kissed his niece and his new sister again. "Welcome to the family. Get some rest."

Brian ushered Matilda back into the waiting room.

"I really need to go home," she asserted. "My head is fine."

"Let me ask Molly first."

"No, I'm good."

"Matty, thank God!" Her brother filled the doorway. He strode toward her, wrapped her in his meaty arms and then held her at arm's length, peering at her face, brows pinched. "You hurt your head. Are you OK? I saw your car wrapped around the tree and the tow truck driver said the police took you here."

"I'm fine, Shamus. Really. But I'm so glad to see you." She buried her aching head in his expansive chest. "Can you take me home?"

"Shouldn't you wait and have the doctor look at your cut?" Brian asked.

"No need. I can patch myself up. Please send me the bill for the repairs on your car." She handed Brian a business card. "Thank you for introducing me to your family."

Matilda addressed the clan, "Congratulations everyone."

****

Matilda strolled down the hall leaning against the burly man's arm as Joe approached Brian from the other direction.

Joe stared at their retreating backs. "Who's that?"

"I don't know. Maybe her boyfriend," Brian replied.

"A boyfriend? Doesn't he mind you dating his girl?"

"I already told you guys it wasn't a date," Brian bristled.

"Don't bite my head off. I didn't hear you. Tell me again, then. You were bringing her to the wedding?"

"She hit my car when I was on my way to the church. Told me she was looking for me. She gave me a letter from Jake."

"Jake, as in Jake Ashford? The missing kid?"

"I didn't make the connection. Could be." Brian slipped a hand into his breast pocket for the letter.

"Let me see it." Joe held out his hand.

About to give Joe the unread letter, Brian

changed his mind. "Not now. Go be with your wife and baby. I'll look it over and we'll talk tomorrow."

Chapter 2

"What? You couldn't spring for the real thing, you cheap SOB?" Nagle bellowed.

"Yeah. I could go for a nice *Cohiba*, Sullivan," Nick chimed in.

"Eat your chocolate cigars and call it breakfast, you vultures," Joe parried out of the corner of his mouth, his long "real thing" cigar teetering in a broad grin.

Brian smiled as Joe advanced toward his desk, the proud new daddy, doling out pink foil wrapped cigars to the men, fellow homicide department members.

"Hey there, pops," Brian greeted Joe.

"Hey, unc."

Joe leaned a hip on the corner of Brian's desk and held the open cardboard box toward him. "Help yourself." He winked his eye and leaned closer to Brian, "I have a box of *Fuente Opus X* in the car reserved for the family. Walk out with me and I'll give you one, OK? "

"Sure." Brian leaned back in his chair, grinning, Joe's happiness contagious. Hard to believe this beaming man was the same guy as the sullen pain in the ass he was a few months ago. "Get any sleep last night?"

"Not a wink, too excited." Joe deposited the cigar box on the desk, unwrapped one, bit the chocolate cylinder half off and chomped. "And I missed Bobbie," he continued around rolling chews. He popped the rest of the candy in his mouth. "If Emma checks out with the pediatrician, I can take them home late afternoon. Even though she's three weeks premature, so far she's doing great."

"That's good, Joe. Congratulations again."

"Thanks, bro." Joe stood up and eyed the box. "Keep those for the next shift. I've gotta get going. You want that *Fuente* now?"

"No, that's OK. I'll catch up with you later. But can you hang on a minute? I'd like your opinion of the letter Matilda gave me yesterday. "

"Sure." Joe rounded the chair at the side of Brian's desk and sat down. He bent his head over the paper Brian handed him.

"Only references the name Jake once," Brian commented while Joe read. "The argument jibes with Alexis Ashford-Whitman's account of the last time she saw her son. The original APB bulletin for State Troopers referenced a Harley motorcycle. Jake Ashford did enroll at Southern Illinois in Carbondale—fits with the downstate reference. No idea what that last 'secret code' part means. Gibberish."

"Uh huh." Joe raised his head, lips scrunched. "Pretty oblique, all in all."

Joe stood up, paper in his hand, arm outstretched. Brian grabbed the letter. "My opinion, Bri, is round file this one and have a nice day. We'd be opening up a huge can of worms if we reopened this as a missing persons case. We've been looking for a body for almost six months."

Brian nodded. "I know. I know. But Matilda was right about Jimmy. She was right that you and Bobbie weren't at the church yesterday. "

"True. But the politics in this case will bring down a shit storm on us if we move on anything other than rock, solid leads."

"You're right." Brian made a fist around the paper and crumpled it in a ball. "Words that appear in Matilda Connors' head don't qualify as rock solid."

Brian flexed his wrist to launch the wad of paper toward the trashcan. Joe gripped his hand before he could.

"Did you just say Matilda *Connors*, Bri? *The* Matty Connors? Jesus, Brian, why didn't you tell me her last name?"

"Connors. Thought I had. So what?"

"Ah, shit. Flatten out that letter. We have to show it to the parents." Joe planted his knuckles on Brian's desk and faced him. "Haven't you ever heard of Matty Connors and the Firing Squad Rapist case in California? Made national news four or five years ago. Danny even teaches a class about it at the Academy—Police Cooperation with Clairvoyants. Connors has never been wrong."

"That guy she left the hospital with yesterday did call her Matty." Brian furrowed his brow, unfolding the letter, smoothing it out on a clear spot on his desk. "So we move on this?"

"Yeah. I hate it, but we have no choice. Sounds like he's alive. The mother has been through hell. Call her and Whitman and say we have something we want them to read. Leave it at that. Let me get over to the hospital and check on my girls. Call me if you set up an appointment and I'll meet you."

****

An evergreen aroma permeated the mansion like they had embarked down a woodland path instead of a Persian-carpeted hallway. Pine-scented air in the foyer and wafts of forest glade cologne trailed James Whitman who led them into the interior of the house. More heated pine aromas circulated from flickering candles on the coffee table in the sunroom where Alexis Ashford-Whitman sat waiting for her husband to usher Brian and Joe to their seats.

"Mrs. Ashford-Whitman, thank you for meeting with us," Brian said after shaking her smooth, stick-thin hand.

Her pale skin framed dove gray eyes, widened huge with anxiety, her body tremors a palpable thing over the coffee table from where Brian sat next to Joe on a sofa.

"As I said on the phone, I don't want you to get your hopes up that this is significant, but we have an...unusual document for you to review." Brian slipped the creased letter out of the pocket of his blazer. "I didn't mention that we have reason to suspect it *might* be a communication from your son."

She rocked in a swoon, her hand trembled and the paper sailed out of her grasp, onto the coffee table.

"Lexxie!" James Whitman hastened to the sofa and clasped his wife's shoulders, bolstering her from behind. He leveled accusatory eyes on them over her head. "I'll have your jobs yet, detectives," he growled.

"Jim." Mrs. Ashford-Whitman crooked her elbow backward and patted his hand. Her woeful eyes pierced Brian, cheeks flaming, gaze unwavering, and then she inhaled deeply. "Could you please bring me my reading glasses, Jim?"

Whitman complied while he stared the Sullivans down. He handed the glasses to her as Brian picked up the letter and extended it towards her. She glanced down and tears welled. Shifting her eyes up, she said, "Yesterday was my birthday."

Eyes downcast again, she continued to read, nodding occasionally while tears tracked her cheeks. On a gasp she uttered, "Kachoom Bombay! My God, Jim, my God. Look at this!" She thrust the letter toward her husband.

"Read the next to the last sentence." Her breathing erratic huffs, she cupped her jaws with open fingers, staring stricken at her husband who scanned the letter and cast her a vacant look.

"He's alive!" She faced Brian, sobbing, laughing, the hope in her eyes pinning him to his seat. "Where did you get this? Where did you get this letter from my Jake?" Her voice vamped up to a screech like a volume dial turned slow, faster, and then yanked to full throttle.

"Jake didn't write the letter..."

"Yes, he did!" she exclaimed. "Kachoom Bombay was the stranger-danger code we used when he was a child. He had a lot of nannies..."

"Drove them away on average once a month from what I hear," Jim Whitman chimed in sarcastically.

"Anyway," she speared her husband with a tight-lipped glare. "Anyone he didn't know who came to pick him up at school or at a friend's house had to supply him with the code. I can't believe anyone but Jake would direct those words to me. He wrote this letter."

"We believe he might have *conveyed* the letter to a woman named Matilda Connors," Brian explained.

"Maybe you've heard of Matty Connors in connection with a publicized case in California?" Joe asked. "She's clairvoyant."

Alexis shook her head, confused.

Brian handed her Matilda's business card. "She told me she saw Jake's words in her head and wrote them down exactly. He didn't supply his last name, but she sought me out specifically to deliver the letter," he related. "We've worked with her on another case and her vision, or whatever you label it, is uncanny."

"I'm convinced this is a communication from Jake. We have to find him. *You* have to find him. I don't care what it takes," she declared, her chest heaving.

"On the basis of this letter we don't have enough..."

"You do whatever it takes," Whitman punched the order at Brian, his tone laden with authority.

Brian and Joe rose from the sofa in unison, the dismissal clear. "I'll contact Ms. Connors to consult on the case. We'll do everything within our power to investigate this."

"Thank you, Detective Sullivan." She handed the business card back to Brian and shook his hand gently. "May I keep this letter?"

"Yes, ma'am. I have a copy in the file. We'll see ourselves to the door."

Outside on the blue stone pavers fronting the Ashford mansion, Brian suggested, "Let's move our cars out of the community before we talk. Pull over outside the security guard's gate for a couple minutes before you go to the hospital."

Joe nodded and the brothers slammed the doors of their respective cars closed. Brian parked at the designated area first, cut the engine and sidled over to Joe's car as he pulled next to him. Joe's window slid open.

"I can't get that Christmas tree smell out of my nostrils. Tastes like I ate pine needles for breakfast," Brian quipped.

Joe snorted.

"How the hell will this whole letter thing play out?" Brian pinched the bridge of his nose, kneading the spot where the headache throbbed most. "There's nothing concrete to investigate."

"We have to go to Matty Connors. Can you handle contact?" Joe asked. "I'd like to get to the hospital now."

"I guess we have no choice. I'll take care of it." Brian tapped the hood of Joe's car. "Go bring your new family home."

****

Through a side window, Matilda spied the nose of Brian's jeep as it emerged through the clearing, tires crunching gravel along the pie-shaped parking apron out front. Sure that his visit to her clinic was official, icy dread coursed through her. Matilda held the wiggling pup securely with one hand atop the metal table, the familiar antiseptic fumes pinching her nose, and punched the wall intercom button with the other hand.

"Shamus, can you please come to room three for a sec? I need you to examine Bootsy for me."

"Sure, Matty. Be right there," came Shamus' booming bass voice.

Seconds later, Shamus took over and Matilda left the room to deal with Brian Sullivan, misgivings colliding in her head. She trudged through the narrow, meandering hallways of the old Victorian toward the parlor-turned-waiting-room in the front of the house, feet weighted down with regrets. *Why did I start this up again? Haven't I suffered enough?*

Brian scuffed through the door, triggering the bell to tinkle overhead as he filled the doorframe. A blast of attraction to the man eroded her opposition to further interaction with him as a crime investigator. His sun-streaked, wind-blown hair touched the arc of one eyebrow, the tips of his earlobes and the side of one high cheekbone. His tanned skin heightened the pure white color around sea blue corneas and the perfect teeth his smile exposed. The fit of his sky blue blazer over wide shoulders and a broad chest, the drape of his slate gray trousers accentuated the musculature of his arms, torso and thighs—a fortress that could both shelter and bombard a woman.

Her life, the essence of her spirit, had always centered around her "truths." Truths planted in her conscious and subconscious mind in many forms. She never questioned or analyzed them; they just *were*. Brian's affect on her struck her as her ultimate personal truth, despite what had to be his impersonal, official mission. Truth or not, she had to end any further involvement with him or risk creating additional nightmares to terrorize her every night. Working with the police again wasn't an option.

"Hi," he said, a single syllable that touched off a concussion of illogical pleasure inside her.

"Hi, Brian," she responded, tamping down the

temptation to hug him hello. "How's the new baby doing?"

"Great, thanks. How's that bump on your head?"

Matilda touched an edge of one of the butterfly strips over her eyebrow. "Turning every color of the rainbow, but it's fine."

He swiveled his head toward the throaty bark of the wolfhound in the corner of the room, then scanned the other occupants in the lounge: primate, feline, porcine, wolfish and human. "Steve told me you're a great vet. Looks like you're pretty swamped here."

"Shamus and I split the patient load," she said.

"And Shamus is?"

"My brother. He came for me at the hospital yesterday?"

Brian's eyes bored into her, a sexy smile twitched the corner of his lips. "Good."

"And 'good' means?"

"The big guy isn't competition. That's good."

"Ah. So we're clear. What competition would that be?"

The sexy smile twitched again. "For but a smile from sweet Matty," he lilted in an Irish brogue.

Squelching an impulse to grin, she molded her face serious and parroted a brogue, "Ah but woe to the knave who plies smiles with an untrue heart."

She grinned now. "What can I do for you, Brian? Did you get an estimate to repair your car?"

"It's about that letter you brought me. It's related to a case. We need your help."

Of course. "I gave you the letter. You know as much as I do." Her heart hammered, nothing to do with the pulse acceleration from earlier flirtation. *I can't go further with this case. No matter what, I have to stay anonymous.*

"I don't know how this thing works with you, but we can give you more to go on."

She shook her head.

"His name is Jake Ashford," Brian persisted.

Her shoulders caved, anxiety quickened and she shook her head more rapidly.

Brian stared at her and rattled off, "His mother is frantic. Her name is Alexis. His stepfather is James Whitman. Jake enrolled as a student at Southern Illinois University. Lived in Carbondale, with a couple—Ben and Jodi. Rode a Harley..."

Dropping her head she squeezed her eyes shut. "I can't. You don't understand. It's impossible."

He grasped her arm and strobes of light flashed on her closed eyelids. This thing she had set in motion could only unleash horror again. She had escaped it when she had delivered Jimmy's message to Brian months ago and had enjoyed her role in solving the case from afar without further involvement. Since California she had honored her truths concealed behind a cloak of anonymity. Why had she shed that cloak with Brian and risked visibility twice?

Matilda blinked her eyes open. His grip on her arm apparently disturbed her patients, inciting barks, screechy meows and grunts from the pig. "Step outside?" A tactical maneuver to position him closer to his jeep and away from her.

As she twisted the doorknob he unlocked the hold on her arm and followed her down the steps, halting by the rear of the jeep. The curled bumper reminded her of her unwise lack of discipline with Brian Sullivan. She had to curtail this now, could not fantasize about this tantalizing man and his appealing family.

"I'd like to help, but there's nothing more I can do," she asserted, absolutely the final word.

"Joe seems to think you can. He's familiar with your work capturing the Firing Squad Rapist," Brian insisted.

Her breath caught in her throat as the execution scene replayed in the recesses of her mind, as it did then and with nightmarish frequency since. *Eric, Eric, my darling. Don't....*

"No, no, no," she chanted, her body quaking.

"What the hell?" Brian threw his arms around her, enfolding her in the fortress that bombarded her with longing and sheltered her from the horror of Eric's death.

Minutes passed as Matilda clung to Brian, weak with released tears, conflicted, wanting both to stay in his arms and disengage. He didn't question her behavior further, didn't utter a sound. The drumbeat of his heart steadied her, the bellows of his chest with each breath, rocked and soothed her. Slowly her tears ceased and the trembling diminished. Her senses deadened with the resolve to refuse further involvement in police work.

She raised her head and met his turquoise eyes, heavy with concern. "I pray the letter helps in the long run, Brian. But there's nothing more I can do."

His arms dropped to his sides. "But..."

Backing away a few paces, "I'm sorry, but that's my final decision." Matilda turned around and advanced toward the steps. Bounding up them, she flung the door open and closed it swiftly behind her, the little bell overhead jangling.

Chapter 3

Matilda braved a glimpse in her dresser mirror and assessed the toll nightmares had etched on her face this time. The cut over her eye had scabbed over. Were those dark circles under both eyes from the accident or lack of sleep?

Her finger traced around the scalloped rim of the framed picture of her and Eric. Smiling, carefree, linked together side by side in the blazing sunshine—foolishly in love and unaware that there wouldn't be a long string of lazy days at that beach in their future. Who could have guessed that three weeks after the picture was snapped Eric would be dead and she would be alone?

Tears welled. *Four years, eight months and twenty-two days without you, and I wish I could stop counting. Maybe then the nightmares would stop.*

Brian Sullivan's request had triggered a cyclone of dreams: Eric-haunted nightmares and Brian-laden fantasies. Dreams featuring Brian admittedly caused most of the tossing and turning last night, but she wouldn't linger on that. If she did, she'd have to acknowledge the heady reawakening of his fantasy kisses, the yearning he stoked in her while defenseless in sleep.

Dreams could be denied and forgotten in daylight. But she couldn't deny how many times thoughts of Brian had upped her pulse and shot suggestive musings through her brain during her routine yesterday. *Why am I letting this happen? Tempting as the man is, I can't risk the danger.*

A red rubber ball bounced against her foot. Clyde clamped his mouth around the ball, lifted it off the ground with a yank of his neck and dumped it again on her foot, demanding her attention.

She stooped and picked it up. "Want to play? Dumb question, right Clyde?"

The Boston terrier cocked his head, trained his screwy eyes at her, dashed out of the room and took off down the hall. Nails clicking against hardwood flooring, Clyde pulled up short, skidded to a halt and turned around toward Matilda, anticipating her toss. Bent halfway out the door, she pitched the ball; he retrieved it, raced back into the bedroom and dropped it on her foot again. The mind-numbing game of fetch continued as Matilda varied the directions she heaved the ball, in the intervals applying her make up and managing to finish dressing. Clyde was Eric's dog. Eric and Matilda would sit for hours in their backyard in California sipping wine, watching the sunset, and throwing the ball for the then frisky puppy until they both ran out of steam—Clyde always won the fetch "endurance" contest.

"OK, kiddo, time to go to work," she commanded.

The dog cast the ball aside and trotted out of the room ahead of her. Matilda followed Clyde as he bolted down the carpeted stairs, scrambled into the kitchen out of view, and then backed out the kitchen door, leading a frail female Boston terrier by a leash attached to its collar.

"Good boy." Matilda squatted down, patted Clyde on the head and placed her hand by the smaller Boston's nose. When the smaller dog's nub of a tail wagged, Matilda picked her up and cuddled her against her breasts.

"Hello, Bonnie."

Bonnie licked Matilda's chin, something she didn't tolerate with any other animal, allowing the dog to use those senses left her. Found after abandonment and obvious abuse, chained in a barn for an indeterminate period of time without food or water, Bonnie was totally blind and deaf. It had taken months before the dog trusted Matilda and Eric enough to show any affection—the "kiss" of her tongue. Clyde, however, had bonded with Bonnie the minute they placed her on the floor next to him, leading and protecting her despite her "old lady" status compared to his puppy-hood.

Matilda grabbed her purse and briefcase before she rushed to the car and strapped Bonnie and Clyde's carriers in the back seat. A quick fifteen-minute commute, then she steered the battered, brown car down the sun-dappled drive, tires treading pebbles noisily. Her window down, she inhaled, relishing the sweet, fragrant air. The painted lady, Victorian home appeared on Matilda's right like a Halloween apparition through the autumn-blazed leaves.

Shamus had wisely convinced their parents, when the property upkeep became too much for them, to hold on to the family home until he was able to secure the financing to buy it. He had converted the bottom floor into a veterinary hospital with offices and moved into the remodeled second and third floors. When Matilda's life had collapsed in California she had been so thankful that she could escape back to this home after her home with Eric had been defiled forever. Shamus had welcomed her here with unconditional love, full partnership in the clinic and tactful respect for her privacy. His heart and arms ever open, she could tell him anything, but he'd never pry. A whiz with mechanical things, he had tinkered her ancient Honda back to life after the accident with Brian. Shamus could fix anything—except his sister.

Since the parking area out front was full, Matilda parked next to Shamus' pick-up in the paved driveway behind the house. Carrying Bonnie with Clyde cantering along side her, Matilda entered through the back door. A cacophony of barks, meows and jungle-like screeches emanated from the presumably packed waiting parlor. Matilda dropped Bonnie off in her office and let Clyde wander around, certain he would find a soft, warm spot for a long nap.

The day flew by with non-stop patients. After tending to the last in her appointment book, Matilda filled her briefcase with files and the journals she intended to go over at home. Kerry, their receptionist, popped in to her office, clutching a file. "Dr. Connors, can you handle a walk-in before you leave? Mrs. Whitman is here with Max."

"Whitman? I don't recognize the name. Isn't Shamus working tonight? Can't he see them?"

"He could, and Max is his patient, but Mrs. Whitman insisted I ask you to treat Max."

"Is it an emergency?"

"The dog looks fine to me. What do you want me to tell her?"

"No problem, sweetie. I'll see Max. Let me have the file, please, and put them in room four. I'll be there in a minute."

"OK. Thanks, doc."

Matilda leaned against her oak desk and flipped through Max's file. A healthy, three year old Labrador, he was up to date on shots and hadn't been in with medical problems since he ate an entire chicken, bones and all, two years ago. Rubbing her hand on the back of her neck, she kneaded stiff muscles. *One more patient, then I can go home and collapse on the bed.*

Matilda opened the exam room door, the dog's file in hand. She forgot her exhaustion at the sight of Max's dark brown pleading eyes as he strained against the taut lead that held him prisoner on the examining table. His tongue lolling, Matilda was sure if he could talk he'd yell, "Get me out of here!"

"It's OK, Max. I won't hurt you." She gently rubbed her hands over his withers and flanks gaining his trust. When he settled down and ceased shaking, she extended her hand to the woman standing next to the table.

"Hi, Mrs. Whitman, I don't believe we've met. How can I help Max today?"

"Max is fine." She shook Matilda's hand firmly. "That's not why I'm here."

"OK..." The backs of her thighs leaning against the exam table, Matilda petted the dog absently. "How can I help you, then?"

"I came to beg you to change your mind. My name is Alexis Ashford-Whitman."

"I'm sorry, Mrs. Whitman, I don't understand."

"I thought you'd recognize my name. My son, Jake Ashford, has been missing for six months. For five of those months, they've been looking for his..." She hung her head, closed her eyes and then jerked her head back up to stare at Matilda, tear-brimmed, gray eyes glistening. "For his body. I thought he was..." She shook her head. "Until I read the letter Jake gave you. The police brought it to me. Forgive me. I'm not making sense I fear. But you have some sort of special connection with my son somehow. This morning I was told you refused to work with the police. Please, *please* reconsider."

Furious that Brian had disclosed her identity to Jake's family, Matilda fought for composure. "I told the police I had nothing to add to their investigation. I'm sorry, Mrs. Whitman, I'd like to help you. But there's nothing further I can do."

"Please call me Lexxie, Dr. Connors."

"I'm sorry, Lexxie. May I walk you to the door? "

The woman's eyes, bottomless wells of pain and grief, beseeched her.

"I have no control over the truths I receive, Lexxie."

"Truths?"

"That's what I call the gifts of vision I receive. I have no control over the revelation or the nature of truths. I can't make them come to me, do you understand?"

"But you worked with the police before and have helped solve cases. How did you control your truths to apply to them?"

Matilda clamped her lips together as bile rose in her throat. Her heart seized and then pounded in escalating, nauseating pulses. She didn't owe this woman, didn't owe anyone the terrible price she had paid. But Jimmy Sullivan had led her to Brian early that year. Her instincts had sent her to Brian with Jake's letter.

An icy hand clamped around Matilda's wrist. "Please, Doctor Connors. I beg you. The police have been working on this case for six months, *six months my baby has been missing!*" Tremors vibrated through the connection of Lexxie's grip on her arm. Tears tracked black mascara rivulets down her cheeks into the corners of her lips. "They have failed to find out where he is or…what happened to him. Every day the first thing I know is Jake's absence. The first thoughts in my head are terrible, terrifying, unspeakable," she keened, her voice rising to hysteria pitch.

Although she wanted to run, turn her back, escape the exam room even more than Max, Matilda couldn't turn her back on this mother's sorrow. "Lexxie, come with me." Covering Lexxie's hand with hers, Matilda nodded assurance gazing deeply into the woman's troubled eyes. "Let's go into my office. I'll take care of Max."

Lexxie dropped her hand away from Matilda's wrist. Turning toward the exam table, she unhooked Max's tether. The dog leaped off the table. "C'mon, Lexxie. Let Max roam. He'll be fine."

Her inbred hostess sensibility had her seated on the loveseat next to Lexxie rather than behind the desk where she presented an authority figure. She didn't want to get sucked into the situation, but she had set this in motion, after all, so she'd see it through.

"I *know* my Jake contacted you. No one could know the words he used other than my son," Lexxie declared. "My husband didn't even know the secret code."

"Jake's father didn't know the secret code?" Matilda asked, surprised.

"My husband is Jake's stepfather. Jake's father died five years ago."

"I'm very sorry."

"Jake couldn't handle his father's death. He took drugs, stole money from my purse. His friends changed and our relationship deteriorated. I offered to pay for counseling, rehab, anything he was comfortable with—repeatedly. But he wouldn't listen. We were not on the best terms when he disappeared. I'm not proud of myself but I threw him out of my home and told him not to come back until he stopped taking drugs, reorganized his life. That is the last conversation I had with my son." She paused, panting, her body shaking so hard against Matilda's arm that the loveseat vibrated audibly along the wood flooring. "I would give anything to have that day back. To return to that moment he slammed the door behind him. He pleaded with me to find him in his letter. I have to figure out how. You heard him, Dr. Connors. You're the only one I can turn to. *Please.*"

Lexxie stared at Matilda, her eyes swimming tears, dark with steely resolve. The woman would never let go until Matilda agreed to this, and Lexxie would win the battle of wills. If she were in Lexxie's position she'd fight just as hard, do the same thing.

"You have to understand that I might not be any help at all." Matilda resigned to whatever fate had involved her with Jake and his mother. "But I'll go through the police file."

Lexxie, crying and laughing, flung her arms

around Matilda's torso, stretched over her lap. "Thank you so much. I can't thank you enough. You're so generous, wonderful."

"Lexxie..." Matilda straightened against the back cushion and trained her eyes into Lexxie's. "Please don't overestimate my control here. This may come to nothing. You *have* to prepare yourself for that possibility."

Lexxie smiled, nodded and clasped both her hands around Matilda's. "I understand, but for the first time since Jake disappeared I feel like I'm doing something constructive to find him and for that I thank you, Dr. Connors."

"You're welcome. And please call me Matilda. I promise I'll do what I can."

The two women rose from the loveseat, hands linked.

"Max!" The dog nosed through the doorway at his mistress' call.

Matilda stooped, hugged him around the neck, and then led them out to the waiting parlor.

"Kerry, please give Mrs. Whitman a box of those peanut butter dog biscuits. Max has a craving for them."

Matilda smiled, said good night and reversed back down the hallway toward the examination room.

Through the open door, a bright splotch of color on the floor under the table caught Matilda's eye. Max had left his red bandanna behind. Matilda bent down to pick it up. The moment she touched it the fluorescent light dimmed and then went black.

The room was cramped with three people in it— two, tall, young men, one sandy-haired and thickly built in a dirty sweat shirt and stale-looking jeans; one slender, raven-haired, well dressed in contrast, clad in pressed slacks and a white shirt. Nothing about the room's location was apparent. The light was low, shadowy—must be nighttime. Crooked vertical blinds on the dark window, a brown, leather ottoman near their pants legs. The other person in the room was a petite, long-haired blonde, pretty, tiny waist, large breasts.

"Hey man, you know I'm good for it," the sandy-haired boy said.

"I want my money today. Now," demanded the other male, belligerently.

"I don't have it, but I'll get it. Cut me some slack, Jake. I'm not pushing you for rent."

"In this dump? Good thing. You've been upping the tab for weeks. I want it. Now."

"Don't hurt him, Ben." The girl grabbed the blond boy by his arm as he lunged toward Jake. *"Please don't hurt him."*

Matilda returned, grasping the edge of the exam table. Deep breathing, she drifted toward her office and sat down hard behind the desk. Unfazed by the fact of the vision itself, she was appalled that she had promised to play an official role in all this. *I have no choice.*

After a quick reference in the phone book for the Windsor Village police station she dialed and asked for Brian.

"Sullivan."

"Hello, Brian. It's Matilda."

"Hi." His inflection registered surprise, delight. "What can I do for you?"

"I'm fine but mad as hell at you."

"Why? What did I do?"

Defensive now. Good. "Why did you give my name to the Whitmans?"

"What were we supposed to do? We had to tell them where the letter came from. You never asked us to withhold your name."

"Mrs. Whitman just left my office."

"I didn't send her there." His tone flat, blunt.

"That's beside the point. She thinks I can help find Jake." Fingering Max's bandana, Matilda gazed out her window at the property's perimeter trees up-lit with spotlights.

"Joe seems to think you can help, too."

Joe's right. "What about you, Brian? What do you think?"

"I'm confused and just as uncomfortable with this as you are. "

"I highly doubt it." She vehemently wished the worst she felt was uncomfortable. *Terrified is more like it.*

"Look. I have no problem with you digging in the file. This case is going nowhere anyway; you can't hurt it. I'll take any help I can get. What did you tell Mrs. Whitman?"

"I told her I would look over the file."

"Good. Thank you."

"There are conditions. I won't do this otherwise," she said urgently.

"O...K..."

"No one knows I'm working on this case outside of you, your brother and the Whitmans. I work entirely behind the scene. No leaks. No press. No one else involved on the police force. It stays between you, me and Joe or I don't help."

"I'll need to tell our commander."

"You do and I will not help. I mean this, Brian. I need your word." She tapped her foot on the floor, a nervous rapid-fire rhythm.

Dead silence on the other end of the phone. Matilda waited, determined not to open herself up to the media madness that surrounds a case. If the press linked her name with this case it was inevitable that her past would be back in the spotlight. That could not happen.

"You have my word," Brian vowed.

"I appreciate that." Exhaling, she wished some of the tension had released with his agreement to her terms. "Can I come to the police station tomorrow to go through the file?"

"I'll be here mid-morning. I'll have everything ready for you."

"I'll be there."

"Great. See you in the morning."

"Brian, one more thing. Jake argued with someone named Ben."

"Ben Jarvis?"

"I don't know. The girl called him Ben."

"The girl?"

"After Mrs. Whitman left I received a truth. I saw three kids, late teens, early twenties. I heard the two guys argue—Jake, Ben and a female voice. The argument was apparently over money. Does this help at all?"

"Yes." His voice dripped with appreciation. "It sure does."

Chapter 4

Half my sibs are married with children. That fact had vaguely disturbed Brian since Emma Jean came home from the hospital and the lot of them had gathered to dote on her at Joe and Bobbie's place. Accustomed to his family's shenanigans, Brian had always genuinely enjoyed everything about them and the role in the family he shared now only with Patrick—the roving bachelor.

His brothers, including Patrick, envied Brian's assumed reputation with women, although they'd never admit it beyond dubbing his dates, Brian's "parade of beauties." If they were in the mood, they'd press him to recount details assuring him they'd be forever guarded from their eagle-eyed sister and straight-laced mother. His unwillingness to part with information about his encounters with the opposite sex had only spurred their belief that he was a lady killer—the fair-haired stud with the perfect smile.

Far from true. He hadn't carved notches on his belt, although if he had, he'd probably need a new belt. Brian had simple friendships now with the women he had dated in the past. No broken hearts bled over him, he had made sure of that. Discovering a new woman was pure enjoyment, exploring with or without boundaries—leaving it up to her. Brian admired women in general. He appreciated the sweetness they brought to his life, needed it. How else could a homicide cop believe that life has any sweetness at all? Single by circumstance, not design, he hadn't thought to give his heart because no woman he'd ever been with had wanted it.

Didn't bother him until recently. Joe's slap-happiness with Bobbie and their daughter had affected Brian. Maybe because of the contrast between Joe's miserable disposition while they pursued Jimmy's killer and his cheerful, almost annoying, sunny personality now. *Any fool could see how happy Kay and Mike, Danny and Molly and now, Joe and Bobbie are. Damn, I think I'm jealous. And turning slaphappy myself thinking about Matilda Connors.*

Brian's arm muscles burned and cut through his reverie. He unclasped both hands from around the chin-up bar and dropped to the floor under his bedroom doorframe. Clad only in boxers, he padded over to his desk, leaned over the chair, tapped the screensaver away on his computer and brought up today's stock quotes. He shook his head. *Thank you, God.* Somehow he had had the intuition to get out on top—his family's investments still intact. A "squirrel" since boyhood with his allowance, newsboy earnings, lawn mowing bucks and income along the way, Brian had assumed another role in the family—financial advisor. How he predicted market fluctuations remained a mystery, chalked up to the explanation that he had a "knack."

Done with reviewing market news, he pulled the chair out from under his desk, sat down and rubbed both eyes with the heels of his hands. He needed caffeine and a shower but his curiosity about an intriguing woman pressed into top place on his list of priorities. He typed "Matty Connors" into the web search box. "Whoa..."

RESULTS 1-10 of about 2,500,000 for Matty Connors.

"You're downright famous, lady."

Scrolling, he clicked links at random and scanned articles.

...body of missing heiress found...Matty Connors'

tip only lead in case...

"Kidnap Victim Leaves Hospital With Parents. ..."We are so grateful to the SFPD and Miss Matty Connors for finding our son. God bless you...."

Visualization Leads Police To Missing Coeds Thought To Be Firing Squad Rapist's Latest Victims.

"That's the one."

Brian moved the cursor and clicked the link.

Three women were found bound and gagged in an RV outside Willets last night according to Captain Judd Tennison, SFPD. The victims, identified as Rose Tilton, Deborah Seneca and Gina Coveny, were abducted from separate state college campuses (Napa Valley University, San Bernadino State Teachers College, Presidio Academy of Art) over the past two week period. Unconscious when the police arrived, Tilton, Seneca and Coveny were flown via medical transport to USFC Medical Center and remain in critical condition. SFPD, working with local authorities, located the RV with the assistance of San Francisco resident, Matty Connors. Ms. Connors, who has worked frequently with the police in locating missing persons, is credited with pinpointing the location of the vehicle at the remote campsite. Ms. Connors, who was not available for comment, is described by an unnamed source as a psychic who visualized the route traveled by the RV driver to its ultimate destination as through the windshield of the vehicle. The person or persons responsible for the abductions were not present at the campsite and remain at large. Captain Tennison neither denied nor confirmed allegations that the three women were victims of The Firing Squad Rapist.

"But Joe said she nailed the guy," Brian muttered. Continuing to scroll down the list, he clicked "next" several times to bring up additional web pages. But the articles were either repetitions of or older than those on the first page. Sliding the cursor up to the query box, Brian typed Firing Squad Rapist.

RESULTS page 1 of 10 of about 4,700,000 for Firing Squad Rapist

"Shit."

Tyler Mullens Faces Trial On Seventeen Counts Of Murder—

Firing Squad Rapist Pleads Not Guilty Based On Insanity—

Policy Deny Undue Force In The Arrest Of Firing Squad Rapist—

"Jesus." Brian rolled his eyes.

Firing Squad Rapist, Mullens Receives Seventeen Consecutive Life Sentences

"More like it."

Book Deal Controversy Continues—Mullens To Sue

"What are you going to spend your advance on in the penitentiary, asshole? Chocolate bars? Fucking nuts."

He scrolled, scrolled and paged forward. On page nine, Brian hit target when he found the headline: Firing Squad Rapist's Last Victim Buried

Eric Quindlen was laid to rest in Heavenly Mother Cemetery today during a private family funeral. The deceased was shot in his home three days ago just prior to the arrival of police on the scene where they apprehended a suspect, identified as vagrant, Tyler Mullens. Mullens remains in police custody awaiting arraignment on the charge of murdering Eric Quindlen. Mullens additionally will be arraigned on sixteen charges of execution style murders and aggravated rape of women ranging in age from seventeen to twenty-five. Eric Quindlen, a second year veterinary medicine student, is survived by his parents and two younger siblings. The Quindlen family requests donations to the Bay Area Animal Rescue Fund in lieu of other remembrances.

Brian scrubbed his hands over his eyes again,

and then let his fingers go lax on the keyboard. Head angled back, he stared at the ceiling while his mind sorted and constructed connections. Peering back down at the monitor, he checked the date of the Quindlen funeral article, deleted his last search input and typed Matty's name in the query box again. A quick reference to the date of the RV campsite article added another piece to the puzzle, but didn't solve it. Eric Quindlen had been murdered the next day.

A veterinary medicine student... He has to be connected to Matty.

Shoving the chair away from the desk with an upward and backward thrust of the back of his thighs, he ambled to the bathroom. A shower might clear his brain some and a quick stop at Starbucks on the way to the station house would take care of the rest.

"Hey, Luci." Brian leaned over the counter and grinned amiably. "Got any specials today? Or should I stick with an *Americano*?"

The statuesque brunette with drool-worthy curves grinned back at him—one of those notches Brian might have carved in his belt a year ago. "Stick with the *Americano*, Bri," she advised as she punched the order into the computer. "Unless you want to pay almost a buck extra for signature hot chocolate or you want to ruin those nice abs of yours with a pumpkin spice latte."

He winked at her and slid his wallet out of his back pocket. "*Americano* it is."

"I'll throw in your favorite syrup." She accepted his money, made change and sidestepped to the coffee bar to make his drink. "Anything new?"

"Joe had a baby girl."

"Really? That's great. Give him a hug for me." Handing him the coffee cup with a forward tilt over the counter, she swung her arm behind the back of his neck and squeezed him tight. "Here's one for you."

****

At his desk in the noisy squad room a half hour before the scheduled meeting with Matilda Connors, Brian had extra time to rummage through the Jake Ashford file and put it in some semblance of order.

Head bent over his file drawer, the edge of his desk cut off his line of vision toward the door, but he knew the instant Matilda entered the room by the rash of sensations only she had ever evoked in him— lost and found. He'd yet to decide whether the conflicted reaction to Matilda could be interpreted as the spell of attraction or witchcraft. *Never felt found before and except for a few stellar moments in a woman's arms, lost? No way.*

The familiar clamor of the squad room abated as if someone pushed a mute button, only distinct to him the click of her heels on the linoleum floor. He raised his head and met penetrating, dark brown eyes, kind eyes that held the warmth of her smile and flashes of acute intelligence. A tortoise shell barrette clasped her thick, honey-colored hair back at the nape of her neck, a soft fringe of layered, glossy bangs streaked with auburn and caramel highlights. She wore little makeup yet her lashes were lush and black.

Brian fixated on the deep maroon lipstick on a damned near perfect mouth.

"Hi," she said.

If he said something, she'd reply and he could watch those luscious lips move some more. "Hi," Brian said, seemingly uninspired.

"I noticed your car in the parking lot. You've got a bungee cord holding on the bumper?" Her eyes danced impishly.

"Does the job. Have a seat. Can I get you anything? The coffee's terrible here, but I'll split my Starbucks with you if you like."

"I'm fine, but thanks." She unbuttoned the quilted, brown car coat she wore over jeans that defined her long, slim legs. Sweeping it off, she draped it over the back of the chair next to Brian's desk. "Ah," she said on an exhalation as she sat down, close enough for him to smell her citrus, maybe grapefruit scent. "I'm good for the repair money, really, Brian."

"I know. I'll get around to it. Are you ready to look over the Ashford file?"

Shadows swept through round eyes, her lips pursed and her face registered something unreadable. "Will you abide by my terms? No one can know about my involvement."

"Don't worry."

"It's absolutely imperative, Brian."

A heightened sheen in her eyes, the threat of tears alerted him to another potential emotional situation. She stared at him—the same look as the preamble to the crying bout outside her office when he could do nothing but hold her until she stopped quaking. He could have pressed her to help with the investigation of the letter despite the waterworks—and would have with anyone else who might have the means to help solve a case. But he hadn't because he had wanted to protect her then, shelter her from whatever had made the tears flow. Now after googling her on the net, the inclination to shield her was even stronger.

I don't give a shit about heat from the Whitmans. I won't hurt her. "I'm not forcing you to work with me, you know. I'm not even sure you can help."

"I promised Lexxie."

Brian furrowed his brow.

"Jake's mom. Mrs. Whitman," she added.

"Oh, right. Funny, I only think of her as hyphenated—Ashford-Whitman. I feel for her, but she's made our lives hell around here. She's very influential in the community and the brass pound lumps on my head after every phone call. Her husband's a royal pain in the ass. All the heat is unnecessary. We want to find Jake almost as much as they do."

"I do, too, Brian. But only if I can remain in the background." She touched his sleeve. "You have to be careful what you disclose about my involvement to Jake's parents, too. Can you do that?"

"You have my word."

Matilda withdrew her hand, locked it with the other in her lap.

"Joe knows who you are, Matilda. From your work in California. It won't go beyond us. Still OK with this?"

"Yes. I am now."

Reaching for the file, he opened it and handed Matilda two photos. "Recognize either of these people?"

With a nod, Matilda returned the photos to him. "I saw both of them. They were arguing with a tall, slim kid with dark brown hair. Called him Jake. Do you have a picture of him?"

"Several." Brian fished through the file and held a snapshot up.

"Yes, that's him."

"The first two photos are of Ben Jarvis and Jodi Wilson, an unmarried couple. Jake was living with the two, according to them, rent-free, until he could find a job."

Matilda nodded her head.

"They claim the last time they saw Jake was two weeks before his mother reported him missing. Professed undying friendship with the kid," Brian continued. "They've been questioned extensively, two or three times separately, then together. Said they weren't worried that he hadn't shown up at their place for a couple weeks. Thought he had shacked up—had done that before. Their stories jibed."

"They didn't appear friendly in my vision,"

Matilda maintained. "Jake demanded money. Ben said, 'I don't have it, but I'll get it.' Then the girl said, 'Ben, please don't hurt him.' I can write this all down for you. Describe what they were wearing, if you like."

"I would, thanks." Brian shoved stuff around his desk until he located a pad of paper.

"I feel kind of conspicuous sitting here in the open," Matilda said, swiveling her head a couple times, a furtive expression in her eyes.

Why does she want to hide? Doesn't matter. Her way or nothing. "OK. Sure." *I haven't seen Joe yet this morning.* "Hold on a sec."

Pushing away from his desk, Brian strode over to Joe's open office door. Empty. Turning back toward his desk, he gestured Matilda over.

"You can use this office. I'd like to bring Jarvis and Wilson in for questioning again. Have you watch from behind the glass. Do you have time?"

Matilda breezed past him into Joe's office. She smelled edible and enticed him with the easy, unselfconscious sway of her narrow hips in butt-hugging jeans. Brian was unsteady on the mystical ground Matilda apparently walked on, but rock solid on station house linoleum in close quarters with a beautiful woman.

She positioned behind Joe's desk and their eyes locked, hers wide, matter-of-fact and seconds later dancing with open appreciation. *Whatever this thing is with her, it's mutual.*

"After you go through the file we could grab a bite to eat until I get Ben and Jodi in here," he suggested.

Matilda smiled, a slow sultry stretching of those gorgeous lips. "Maybe. I can always come back later, rework my schedule if it takes too long."

Duty first. "These two don't seem to be gainfully employed. Supposedly they're students, but they never seem to go to classes, either. The campus is a couple hours away by car. I'll bring you the file. We'll have them in here first thing tomorrow morning. How's that?"

Chapter 5

"Sit down." Joe tapped his hand on the seat of the wood chair next to him.

Brian ignored him and continued pacing around their commander's desk.

"You're driving me crazy. *Sit down.*"

"Sorry." Brian complied for a couple seconds, then sprang up and resumed pacing.

"Why are you so nervous?"

"I promised Matilda I would keep her name out of this." *And I will no matter how much heat I get.*

"Why the hell did you do that?"

"It's the only way she would stay on the case and help us."

"Shit." Joe stood, marched to the window, tugged the blinds up and opened it. A cold breeze lowered the room temperature. "What are you going to tell Caprisi?"

The office door banged against the jam and Commander Caprisi bustled in, a cell phone jammed between his shoulder and his ear, a stack of files in one arm and an extra large coffee mug in the other.

Brian and Joe sat down on the chairs in front of the desk and waited for their boss to settle down in his seat behind it.

"Explain to me why I should OK pouring more department resources into a cold case." Caprisi tented his fingers and stared at Brian.

"We have new information. Could be Jake Ashford is alive," Brian suggested.

"What the hell?" Caprisi knitted his brow and squinted at Brian. "What kind of information?"

"A letter sent by Jake to his mother," Brian

responded.

"When?"

"Less than a week ago in time for his mother's birthday." Brian extracted a copy of the letter from a file folder in front of him on Caprisi's desk and handed it to his commanding officer.

Caprisi scanned it, then glared at Brian with the full force of higher rank intimidation. "It's been verified?"

"Mrs. Ashford-Whitman is convinced her son sent the letter."

"Where did you get it?" he barked.

"We can't tell you."

Caprisi's face reddened and Brian held his stare. "You'll tell me or get out of my office."

"Our source wants to remain anonymous or no dice with any more leads," Brian asserted.

Caprisi leaned back in his chair, arms folded, eyes on the ceiling. "You've had this case—what is it now? Six months?"

"Yes sir."

Caprisi lowered his head slowly and glared at Brian again. "And this letter just turned up?"

"Trust me on this one."

Caprisi's hooded eyes switched between Brian and Joe, then back at Brian. "You have three weeks. That's it."

On his feet at the begrudging nod of his superior officer to do things his way, Brian focused on Joe, flicked his head toward the door. "Thanks, sir. You won't regret this."

"I better not," Caprisi said to their backs as Joe followed Brian's lead and they scrammed out of the office.

He slugged his brother on the shoulder. "Thanks for all the support in there, Joe."

Joe didn't flinch. "Hey, it's your case. I am just a fresh eye. What's next?"

Sauntering with his brother toward Joe's office,

Brian replied, "I'm putting Matilda behind the glass when Jarvis comes in. Maybe something will come of that."

"You don't sound too confident about it," Joe remarked.

"I'm not. I don't think she can force any of her woo-woo."

Joe belly laughed. "Woo-woo? Is that a scientific term?"

"You know what I mean. I don't want to spend the next three weeks waiting for Matilda to come up with...truths...or whatever. You're the reason I put this in motion with the mother."

"You've researched her track record." Joe checked a couple phone message slips on his desk and Brian hung back leaning a shoulder against the door jam. "She doesn't disappoint. Her record's perfect."

"I know but there's always a first time."

"Give her a chance, Bri."

"I am. But there's something under the surface with her. I don't know. I'm worried about her."

That prompted a slug in the shoulder from Joe. "Going soft over a pretty face, huh?"

He issued his opinion of the insinuation with a roll of his eyes. "Yeah right."

Joe chuckled. "Find me when you're ready to start questioning Jarvis. I'll help. I have a few phone calls to make and I want to check in with the girls."

"How is my godchild doing?"

Joe's face transformed like Brian had flipped on the "joy" switch with the simple question. "She is amazing. Slept through the entire night last night. Bobbie and I kept looking in the cradle to make sure she was all right. I could stare at that child for hours."

"How is Bobbie feeling?"

"Almost back to normal. I could stare at that woman for hours."

Brian smiled. "You've got it bad, bro."

Joe slugged Brian in the shoulder again. "Try it some time."

Refusing to rub his arm, Brian asked, "Are you going to Kay's for Halloween?"

"Wouldn't miss it. Let me make those calls."

****

Matilda sat, white knuckled hands grasping the steering wheel, eyes fixated on the brick building in front of the car. Anxiety kept her frozen to the seat. Why had she allowed herself to be dragged back into this world? Jake's mother deserved to know her son's whereabouts, but why did she have to be the one to find him?

Before she gave in to the impulse to shift into reverse and beat a hasty retreat, she jerked the key out of the ignition and rapidly exited the car. Her stiletto boot heels clicked along the concrete pavement fronting the police station. Pushing through the glass door, she stepped up to the desk.

"Hello again, miss," Officer Nagle greeted her, his face alight with recognition.

"Hello, .Officer Nagle. Detective Sullivan is expecting me this time." She smiled, remembering her first encounter with this man. Without much to go on when she had tracked down Brian after Jimmy Sullivan's ghost had "visited" her—only Jimmy's name and a photo of Brian in uniform—this officer had acted like she was certifiable at their first introduction.

"I'll get Sullivan up here." Nagle stepped out from behind the desk and opened the squad room door wide on its hinges, his mouth in an O, presumably to holler. But Brian already wound his way through the desks toward her.

With his long, powerful strides, Brian bridged the gap between them in seconds. Still it was enough time for her earlier questions to evaporate, insignificant. *You should know by now not to question where truths lead.* Matilda enjoyed the long, dormant, sexual zingers that Brian's powerful movements set off inside her and forgot her skittishness in the car.

"Hi…" Brian clamped his lips down on an "em" sound, flicking his eyes at Nagle.

Matilda returned his sheepish grin with a broad smile, acknowledging his intention to keep the commitment of confidentiality surrounding her involvement with his case.

"Come on in." Brian flattened his long frame against the door. She crossed the threshold in front of him, paused so he could take the lead position and then silently followed him to an elevator in the back of the squad room.

"The interrogation room is on the second floor," Brian imparted as he punched the up call button.

While she waited, Matilda's mind went pleasantly blank, registering only the chipped paint on the elevator doors and Brian's enticing all-male, shower soap and spice scent.

The elevator doors parted with the whine of braking metal and opened. A pretty blonde glanced at Matilda absently, then at Brian with wide-eyed attention. "Hey, Brian. How's it going?"

"Hey, Sherri. Good and you?"

"Fine. Call me." She sashayed past Brian, giving Matilda a pointed once over and continued through the squad room.

Matilda and Brian replaced the blonde in the elevator. Unreasonably stung, Matilda inquired, "She your girlfriend?"

"Just friends." Brian leaned across Matilda and pushed the button to close the doors.

Good. He radiated heat, apparently contagious. Her pulse skittered from more than nerves over the criminal investigation.

On the second floor Matilda followed Brian down the institutional-like corridor, slightly nauseous, her stomach muscles clenching. Worn carpeting tamped down with footprint tracks, soiled in the middle, dark scratches on off-white walls, she'd treaded virtually identical halls and the familiarity wasn't comforting. Brian turned through an open doorway at the end of the hall and switched on soft lights after he ushered Matilda inside the room.

"Make yourself comfortable." He pointed to one of the armchairs in a row facing a wall of navy blue curtains. Matilda perched on the edge of the seat, her hands in her lap clenching the suede material of her skirt.

"Would you like something to drink? Coffee, tea or water?"

"No thanks."

"Are you OK? You look pale."

"Honestly? I almost pulled back out of the parking spot. But I gave my word. I'll follow through."

"Thank you. I really appreciate it. I'll try and make it quick. Ben Jarvis is in the room with Joe. Jodi Wilson isn't here today. She's out of state visiting with relatives, but she'll be back next week if you feel you need to see her in person. We can address that after you see Ben. Since the last time we pulled them in, they left school and moved back to this area." As he talked, Brian drew the curtains open, arms overhead, tugging each panel from the middle to the sides.

One-way glass covered half the wall behind the curtains. The belligerent young man stared at the glass. Matilda flinched and retreated as far as the chair back permitted.

Leaning down, Brian rubbed the top of her shoulder lightly. "Don't worry. He can't see you."

She smiled up at him, at the mild comfort of his touch, "I know, Brian. I've done this before. I know the routine."

"Let's begin then. There's a direct line to the room." He pointed to the phone next to her chair. "If you need me just buzz." Brian hesitated then left the room, closing the door behind him.

Smoothing her skirt over her knees, she took a deep breath in a vain attempt to regulate her breathing, her heart beating erratically.

While she studied Ben's face intently, a door opened, closed and Brian entered the scene. He took the seat next to Joe, their backs to Matilda, and in a deep baritone, a sound that triggered lovely, distracting sensations through her, addressed Ben across the table, "This session is being taped. You have been read your rights and waived your right to have a lawyer present. Is that correct?"

"Yeah. I know my rights. I don't need a lawyer because I didn't do anything wrong. Why can't you guys leave me alone?" Ben sneered, all tough guy veneer.

"When was the last time you saw Jake Ashford?"

"I told you guys a million times. A couple weeks before the end of second semester. Everyone thinks Jake was perfect. He wasn't. He was fried half the time. It wasn't fun anymore. But I really liked the dude. We were friends since we were kids. He must have shacked up and I figured, good. Let some time pass and then look him up again. He never came back to the trailer. When we found out he was missing, I checked around. Nobody knew where he was. After the summer Jodi and I left and moved back here."

Brian shot up, his face inches away from Ben's. "Can't help but notice you're using the past tense, pal," he spit out angrily.

A slight shift in Ben's posture, but he stared at Brian defiantly.

Easing back into his seat, Brian asked in a conversational tone, "Has Jake contacted you?"

"No." Ben stared straight at Brian, lips pursed.

Then he slouched in his seat and looked at the table as if bored.

"You sure? He contacted his mother recently."

Ben's head jerked up, eyes huge, disbelieving. *Hopeful?* "That's great man. Where is he?"

"You tell me." Brian was in Ben's face, his body leaning to the right, obviously careful not to obstruct her view.

Ben's nose an inch away from Brian's, lips curled, the kid snarled. "Back off, man. What part of *I don't know* don't you cops get?"

Rearing back, Brian opened a file on the table in front of him and angled it out of Ben's view. Referring to the file and then turning up toward Ben he continued questioning, "The last time you saw Jake, did you argue?"

"No." Ben's eyes shifted left, and then his head turned in the same direction away from what had to be the heat of Brian's glare.

"Look at me."

No reaction.

Crack! Brian's fist pounded down on the table. "I said look at me and answer that question. Did you argue?"

Ben's eyes downcast, he jiggled his right leg. "Yeah, we argued. He owed me money and I wanted it. I needed it."

"To buy drugs?"

"Yeah. OK. To buy drugs." A shrug of his shoulders. "But I've changed. I came home. Cleaned up and I went back to school. I'm trying to get my life back, man. Can you guys leave me alone?" He buried his head in his arms on the table.

"I want my money. I am sick and tired of your fucking excuses. I need it."

"I'll get it."

"When? I need it today."

"I can't get it today, but I will get it."

"Don't, Ben, don't shoot him."
"What the hell? Don't point that at me!"
"It's my old man's. I can pawn it, get the money."
"What are you, fucking crazy?"
A gunshot cracked inside Matilda's head as if her brains had exploded.

Matilda rammed against the back of her chair knowing objectively that what she'd just heard pertained to Jake and the kid in the interrogation room...not Eric. As much as she struggled to grab onto the present and stare through the one-way glass, the past clutched at her and she relived her personal nightmare.

She sat in a similar room at the California police department going over files when she heard the gun shot. The file slipped from her hand. She was too late. The horror of finding Eric slumped on the floor in their kitchen, the blindfold tied over his eyes. Bonnie and Clyde slipping in Eric's blood, pooled on the tile floor.

Tears streamed down Matilda's cheeks as she picked up the phone to buzz Brian. He glanced at the glass, stood and answered the phone on the wall of the interrogation room. "Sullivan."

"He's dead."

"What?"

"I heard the gun shot. Jake is dead."

Brian hung up the phone and addressed Joe, "I'll be right back."

"Did you see Ben shoot him?" Brian asked as he walked through the door. He stopped short with a glance at Matilda's face, his eyebrows knit.

"What happened? Are you all right?" Kneeling in front of her, he clasped her cold trembling hands. "I'm so sorry I put you through this. I didn't realize how it would affect you."

Some warmth flowed from his handhold, penetrating the icy memory of Eric's death. "It's kind of complicated."

His eyes darkened, his face creased with concern.

"I might not look it, but really I'm fine," Matilda assured him.

Tightening his hands around hers, more sweet comfort banished the nightmare echoes in Matilda's head.

"I didn't understand you had such dramatic responses to your truths."

"Not always. I'm sorry to be so emotional." She forced a weak smile, still intending to reassure Brian that she could handle this and maybe convince herself.

"Don't apologize. We don't have to continue. Let me take you home." He unfolded from a crouch and dropped her hands with the motion.

She smiled up at him, calmed by his willingness to consider her feelings. "I don't need to go home. Let me tell you what I heard."

Listening intently, his teal eyes steely with concentration as Matilda recounted the exchange, Brian stared down at her. "Did you see Ben shoot the gun?"

"No, I didn't. I heard the argument, I heard the girl plead, then Jake's voice, 'don't point that at me,' and then a gun went off. I knew Jake was dead."

"How?"

"That I don't know. I didn't see any of this. I sense that he's dead and I'm positive you should continue to look for his body. Not a live, missing person."

Brian sat heavily in the chair next to Matilda's.

"And knowing Jake was dead caused you to break down?"

Chewing on the corner of her lips, a shimmer of revulsion coursed through Matilda at the memory. "Not exactly. The gunshot triggered a personal response. It had nothing to do with the case."

"Tell me about it."

She shook her head. "I can't. At least, not now."

"You can trust me."

"I know." Matilda inhaled and exhaled deeply. "I just can't talk about it right now."

"I have to let Ben go. Hearing a gunshot is not enough to hold him." Brian picked up the phone.

"Let him go, Joe. I'll tell you later. Yeah, thanks." Brian stood and yanked the curtains closed.

His back to her, his body rigid, she read the language. "You're disappointed with me."

Turning around he gave her an appreciative smile. "No. I'm not at all. Just frustrated that we can't pin anything on that kid. I suspected all along that he killed Jake. Even with this new information, we can't make a charge stick."

"Do you want to bring in Jodi next week? It might trigger something," she suggested.

"Are you up to it?"

"I will be. I gave my word to help with this case and I will."

"Thanks." His expression brightened. His grin shot devilish glints in his eyes and dimples in his cheeks. Extending a hand to her, she placed hers atop his and her palm seemed to fuse with his skin, melting, a spiking heat pulsed through her.

"Do you have time to go and grab a cup of coffee and something to eat?" Brian invited.

Matilda checked her watch, a pretense, because the only word that occurred to her in the thrall of Brian Sullivan's tantalizing presence was, yes. "I have office hours this afternoon, but a cup of tea would really hit the spot."

Brian put his arm around Matilda's shoulders, spreading an enveloping warm "shawl" across her back. Pampered by his protective hold, she left the room and retraced the steps back to the second floor elevator.

A female officer, brunette, pretty, with a confident, loose-limbed gait, approached them in the opposite direction. "Hi, Brian."

"Hey, Jen. How's the arm?"

"Coming along. I'll be ready when the season begins. You can count on me."

"Great. See ya later."

Matilda tilted her head up and shot a questioning look at Brian.

"Jen's the pitcher on our softball team. She's great. We need her to beat the fireman this year. And—"

"I know," she interrupted. "She's just a friend."

Chapter 6

The belly-busting punch of attraction muddled Brian's senses. A shapeless, dull brown, car coat over a down-to-the-calves suede skirt with boots covering any remaining scraps of leg hardly accentuated Matty's body, especially in contrast to lush Luci, the barista. Matty. That's who she was to him now. Maybe the reason stemmed from all those articles referring to her nickname, or because thoughts of her now had become more personal for him.

In profile at the Starbuck's café counter she reminded him of the Irish colleens in his extended family: long, dark blonde hair, ultra fair skin, a thick sweep of curled eyelashes, pert upturned nose and the requisite smatter of freckles across its bridge— sort of an elongated, negative of his platinum blonde, Irish through and through sister, Kay. But the almond shaped, cocoa-colored eyes that turned to him, amused, hinted of more exotic locales than the Emerald Isle—a Turkish principality, a Mayan village, a Greek Isle? Mysterious, exotic Matty drew him like a beckoning Sirens' song.

"How do you ever decide what to drink here?" Her upturned face was mere inches away from him, imminently kissable.

Resisting the where-the-hell-did-that-come-from impulse to bend closer and taste her lips or slip his arm around her waist for the sheer pleasure of physical connection, Brian scrutinized the menu instead. His cheeks warmed uncharacteristically when he realized Luci assessed him knowingly from behind the counter.

"Do you like coffee or tea or neither?" Luci posed the question to Matty.

"Tea."

"You've never been to a Starbucks before?" Considering that there were ten of them in a five-mile radius from this supermarket store, Brian didn't think it possible.

"Nope." Matty eyed the baked goods' display case. "I don't drink coffee and figured what's the point?"

"Try the Chai Latte," Luci instructed scooping up a tall cup. "We'll start you with the smallest size and let the addiction take root slowly." The barista winked at Brian, who for once hadn't a clue what Luci was saying with the body language.

"One of those, too, please." Matty pointed to a pastry. Couldn't be gooier.

"A woman who isn't always on a diet. That's what I like to see," Brian declared and then he gave Luci the nod to make him his second *Americano* of the day.

Weaving through the tables to one by the window, they set their cups down and she shrugged out of her coat, hanging it on the back of her chair. Her snug cotton sweater hiked up with the motion exposing a ribbon of creamy skin over the waistband of her skirt. Very appealing. Then it was gone from his view when she plopped down in the seat across from him and he promised himself he'd figure a way to see that and more sometime soon. They dug in—she with gusto into the confection and Brian with pensive sips on the tongue-scalding brew.

Too late for breakfast and early for lunch crowds, they had the café area to themselves. Spicy smells from the nearby supermarket bakery permeated the air, a homey coziness that distanced Brian from one-way windows and interrogation rooms. He hoped it did the same thing for her.

Dabbing her lips with a paper napkin she came

up for air. "I didn't know Dominick's markets had these little restaurants. This is nice. Thank you for suggesting this. And thanks for the treat."

"Sure. You don't shop here? It's about five minutes from the animal hospital."

She shook her head and swallowed another bite before replying, "Uh-uh. I live in central Windsor Village near the leg of the Prairie Path by the railroad station. I have a townhouse. You know the Jewel supermarket downtown?"

He nodded. "Nice area. I live off Briarcliffe Boulevard. In a condo. When I don't live at the station house, that is," he said wryly.

"I know what you mean. I've been doing double shifts at work all summer to give Shamus occasional breaks. There seems to be no end to ailing critters." She smiled, cocked her head, a glint in her spellbinding eyes. "You seem to find time for socializing, though. In the space of an hour I think I've been introduced to three women distinctly coming on to you."

Wracking his brain at her bemused grin he could only come up with two. "Sherri and Jen?"

Matty tossed her head toward the coffee counter. "And that lady there."

"Oh. Luci. Yeah, well. You're pretty perceptive."

Her laugh was as full of gusto as the way she had demo'ed her pastry. "Lack of perception has never been one of my problems. Quite the ladies man, aren't you, Detective Sullivan? Seems like you're all over the map."

"I've covered my share of territory." He sipped from the cup again and gazed appreciatively at her bratty but cute expression. "And you, Miss Connors? Probably broke hearts from coast to coast, I'll wager."

Her eyes clouded and skittered away from his. *Damn. Put my foot in my mouth.*

"Matty…" He clasped her hands so he felt her

body flinch. "Is it OK if I call you Matty? Nothing I read about you used your full name."

Taken aback, she extended her arms straighter, her face further away. But she didn't slap his hands off hers, which he took as a good thing. "You've been reading about me?"

"Internet. I googled you," he admitted.

"Huh." The full force of those mesmerizing eyes beamed at him. "Then you know. I don't have to rehash anything."

"Frankly, I don't know squat about you. Your gift or truths? I don't know what to think. But you're right, you don't have to rehash anything with me if you don't want to."

The sweetness that flowed from her linked hands to his fingertips and that bored into him from her tender doe eyes swelled his heart. Her open, vulnerable expression made him eager to know every detail about her past while simultaneously urging her to withhold it to protect her from the ugliness those Internet articles covered.

****

"I want to tell you everything. I think I'm meant to." No huge revelation involved, but her intuition nudged her forward. *Maybe Brian is destined to be my nightmare-slayer. All I know is that he's the receiver of my truths for a reason. That vision of him in his tuxedo. I thought he was my groom.*

"But before I talk about my history, I want to tell you about something more current," Matilda continued. "The morning I rammed your car? Had that truth from Jake?"

He nodded, a quizzical expression furrowing his eyebrows.

"I came to find you specifically with the letter because I saw you."

"Where?"

"Walk out your front door."

Elbow on the table, his chin in his hand, Matilda

glanced at the bulge of his bicep. *The man makes my head spin.*

The furrow in his brow deepened. "I don't follow. You were outside my place?"

"No. I was home. I saw you in a tuxedo. Just a flash. So I picked up the letter and got in my car. I honestly didn't know where you were. Just had faith that I'd find you."

"Sure as hell did," he said with a headshake and a chuckle. "You do realize how weird this is?"

Matilda smiled demurely. "Gets weirder but I'll tell you about that some other time. OK..." Withdrawing her hands from his, she folded them on the table in front of her and took a steadying breath. The door to her right opened ushering in the sound of tramping feet and a breeze of autumn crisp air that bolstered her. "My grandma's name is Pearl. She and grandpa had two children, my mom, Mavis and my Uncle Shamus—my brother is his namesake and we're Mom's only children. I know for sure that the ability to see truths goes back to my Grandma Pearl and skipped the generation in between. Pearl says her grandma had the gifts, too. She told me that my visions are much more vivid and frequent than hers ever were. And more uncontrollable. I started receiving truths when I was in elementary school, really young. I always knew where the other kids were hiding when we played hide-and-seek. I saw them and went straight for them every single time."

"Wow. Kind of makes sense. Get beat up on the playground much?" His lips pursed, a playful twinkle in his azure eyes.

"Funny." She punctuated her sarcasm with a gentle arm-swat. "Actually my ability kept me out of trouble. But mostly all this...perception, added up to a vague sixth sense. Until I started receiving truths about a missing person I learned about watching a newscast. I was in high school. I told my mother about it and she took me to the local police station. That case had a happy ending. For about ten years or so the cases I provided information on all did. If not finding someone alive, at least bringing the bad guys to justice."

Her chest heaved with a deep intake and exhalation. "Well, as I said they all ended happily until I received truths about the murderer the media called the Firing Squad Rapist. That was the last case I consulted on—before I came forward with information from your brother—and it didn't have a happy ending for me. I lost someone very dear to me. My fiancé, Eric—"

"Quindlen," Brian interjected.

She knit her brows, disturbed. "Yes. How did you know that? I thought I succeeded in suppressing that information. Captain Tennison promised..."

"I read his obit. Saw that he was a veterinary medicine student. It wasn't spelled out."

"OK. I'm not the only one who's perceptive." The playful grin she gave him belied the dive of mourning and regret deep inside. "Yes, his name was Eric Quindlen and I saw his death, his execution by a satanic beast named Tyler Mullens, before it actually happened. I didn't know that Eric was really still alive at the time I received the truth. But as it turned out, it was a premonition."

Brian's posture stiffened and his expressive eyes exuded sympathy. Not sure she wanted that from him, or from anybody, she hesitated. She hadn't trusted her family or anyone with the details before now. But her instincts pushed her forward driven by the sudden certainty that she could not only trust Brian, she *should* trust him. *Eric is my past; Brian is my future.*

"Mullens overcame Eric from behind and smashed him against the refrigerator. One of our dogs rushed in and attacked Mullens' leg. He kicked the dog clear down the hall, out of my view."

Staring at her hands clasped in a tight knot on the tabletop, she continued in a quiet monotone, "Then he kicked Eric repeatedly while he lay on the floor and screamed my name over and over. He blindfolded Eric and dragged him up on his knees. He aimed two guns at Eric's head point-blank and fired—his version of a firing squad—then fled out the back door. Our dogs surrounded Eric and licked his face, whining, losing their footing in his blood pooling on the floor around him."

"Matty. Don't. I've heard enough," his voice gruff with concern.

Prying her hands apart, she covered one of his, so warm compared to hers. Courage filled her. "The press had splashed my name everywhere for leading the captain to a campsite and saving three women before Mullens could do the same thing to them. Mullens intended to kill me, but found Eric home. I got the police there in time to capture Mullens and put him away, but it was too late to save Eric. He was buried on our planned wedding day."

Brian arched over the table and slid his hands along her arms to a firm hand-grasp. "I'm so very sorry, Matty. I can't believe you want to help on the Jake Ashford case after all you've been through." Still hanging over the table clinging to her hands he stated firmly, "I won't let you."

"Ah Brian." Swiveling her hands so that her palms molded over the backs of his hands, she smiled up at him. "Thank you for saying that. Sit down, please. I'm all right. Really."

As he complied she studied his face. A slow smile spread on his lips and dimpled his cheeks in response to her smile. His sandy hair shot through with sun streaks framed a ridiculously handsome face. She'd like to see if the summer sun would deepen the light tan on his skin and multiply platinum highlights in his hair. Live the notion that he represented her karma and discover whether the vision of him in his tuxedo foretold his role as a groom rather than his brother's best man. That she had confided the events leading to Eric's murder, dry-eyed, to another living soul carried immense import for Matty. She could no more turn away from working with Brian on this investigation than she could will away the truths that had come to her lifelong.

"I plan to do whatever I can to help you with the investigation, Brian. And although you may not believe me, I'm grateful to you for listening just now. I've never told that story to anyone before and just getting it out makes me feel sort of hopeful."

"Really? Well, OK, that's good."

Several customers clattered to a nearby table, scraping chairs along the floor, chattering.

Not the least self-conscious, Matty enjoyed the hand-link with Brian, a comfortable, dream-like togetherness that somehow fit. Perhaps she projected the sentiments through her eyes because something triggered a hungry glint in his eyes that spoke more of dares than dreams.

Up for dares she asked, "Do you have any policies about dating?"

"Policies? There isn't a handbook or anything."

"I mean," she said, refusing to stammer, "against dating women you work with?"

"Obviously not. You did meet Sherri and Jen." The dimples deepened on his cheeks.

"Good. Maybe you'll ask me on a date sometime?"

"Maybe. I take it you'd like that?"

"I would. And it *is* all right if you call me Matty."

Chapter 7

Brian drove the jeep into the parking lot in front of the row of townhouses where Matty lived, his eyes alert watching for darting trick-or-treaters. *A costume party date!* He laughed at the boyish formality. *When was the last time I took a date to Kay's Halloween bash? Had to be back in high school with Linda. What was Linda's last name? Damned if I can remember.*

A clown, cheerleader and what might be a bowling ball distracted him. He tracked their progress skipping up the path leading to Matty's front door where a cluster of other trick-or-treaters gathered. In their midst, a large mustard bottle stood a head above the other children.

Brian popped on a pair of round, black-framed glasses, swung the car door open and almost fell on his face when his long Harry Potter robe caught on his boot on his way out. Adjusting the robe he proceeded up the path. A small boy dressed as a doctor stood in front of the mustard bottle petting two squirming giant hot dogs.

The mustard bottle addressed him, "Hi Brian. Or should I say Harry?"

"Matty? Is that you?" Somewhere under the pointy, triangular, bright yellow cap and foam bottle costume lurked his sultry, curvy date.

"Yep." The tinkling of her laughter made him smile.

"You look very...yellow." A black and white dog encased in a stuffed fabric, hot dog bun sniffed his shoe.

"Hey buddy." Brian squatted down, extending

his hand for the dog's inspection.

The boy next to Matty "mustard" stooped and picked up the smaller costumed "hot" dog. "This is Bonnie." The dog's tiny, pink tongue licked the boy's chin. "You have to be very careful with her. She's special," the miniature medic asserted.

"What makes her so special?" Brian scratched the larger dog's neck. "This little guy looks special, too."

"That's Clyde. He's a good dog but he's not special like Bonnie. She's deaf and blind. That means she can't hear or see."

"You are very lucky to have such a special dog." Brian stood up and shook the boy's hand. "You're special, too, for taking care of her."

"She's not my dog. She's Doctor Matty's dog. Clyde is, too. But I am a big boy and Doctor Matty lets me take care of Bonnie sometimes. I'm going to be a dog doctor when I grow up."

A dark-haired woman emerged from a neighboring door in the row of townhouses and hurried towards the group, wiping her hands on a dishcloth, an apron knotted around her waist.

"Hey, Brian."

"Hey, Penny."

"Time to bring Bonne and Clyde in for dinner, Owen."

"We're babysitting for Bonnie and Clyde tonight, aren't we, Mommy?" The boy glanced up at Penny, his face glowing with adoration.

"Yes, honey, we are. We will take good care of them and they can sleep at our house. Have a good time, Matty."

"Thanks, Penny."

"Good seeing you again, Brian."

"You, too, Penny. Great kid you got there."

"I know. Thanks."

Brian followed Matty through her front door into a small vestibule. An oval wall mirror reflected back his owlish eyeglasses and signature Harry Potter thunderbolt scar fake tattooed on his forehead.

"Do you know every female in Windsor Village?" She smiled as she took off her bright yellow hat and shook her long hair out seductively.

"Nope, only the pretty ones." Brian snickered at her semi-tolerant frown. "I'm only kidding. I played softball with Penny's husband. I heard the two of them separated."

"Yes, they did and it's so sad for Owen. He misses his dad a lot."

"He worships his mother, and you. I could see it on his face."

"He's a great kid. I like having him around and he has the right touch with my dogs. Come on in."

She closed the door behind him and gestured for him to lead down a narrow hallway that opened into a combined kitchen and family room area. Cardboard boxes were stacked two or three high in a couple places around the perimeter. Only an impressive, flat screen television hung on the stark, white walls with a comfortable looking black couch and coffee table in front of it.

"Great place you have here. When did you move in?"

"Move in? Gosh, I guess about four years ago."

"Four years? Not planning on staying? Afraid to set down roots?"

"Gee, doctor, would you like me to lie on the couch and tell you about my childhood?" Her sarcasm-laced retort slapped him in the face.

"Honey, if I get you to lie down on the couch I don't plan on asking about your childhood." Her posture loosened and her eyes flashed just the right level of interest in the proposition to encourage him.

"My brothers might label me a slob. I say I'm organized differently. I won't criticize your unpacking skills in the future." He grinned. "Truce?"

"Truce." She folded the backs of her hands against what probably were her hips under the mustard bottle and sized him up. "Nice costume. I never would have picked you for a Harry Potter fan."

"Harry and I go way back. When the first book came out I started reading it to my niece, Mary, and hate to admit it, but it hooked me. Of course, if you tell any of my brothers I'll flat out deny it. Sadly, Mary doesn't need me to read to her anymore, but I hope she remembers and likes this costume. I really didn't know many other movie characters."

"Movie characters?"

"Each year Kay picks a theme. This year it's movie characters. Didn't I mention that when I called?"

"I don't think so. Oh no," she lamented, frowning as she glanced at her costume. "What movie do you know that could possibly have a giant mustard bottle in it?" Fanning her fingers over her chin and mouth she lowered her eyes, thoughtful. "OK, I've got a plan. Give me a minute to regroup. Make yourself comfortable. There's a great bottle of wine open on the counter and some cheese in the fridge. Help yourself. I'll be right back." She dashed out of the room.

Brian took a wine glass from the rack above the counter. Hanging an arm over the refrigerator door, he peered inside. Just what he expected. Vegetables, yogurt and a wedge of soy cheese. *No thanks.* He poured a glass of wine, ruby red and berry-chocolate fragrant, and tested it with a sip. *Good stuff. She has great taste in wine. Probably from her years of living in California.*

Comfortable on the couch, he plucked the remote off the coffee table and turned the television on. Surfing the channels he was surprised and delighted that she had all the premium sports channels.

"Sorry I took so long. What do you think of the

wine?"

Brian clicked off the TV at the sound of her voice and stood up as she entered the room. The woman blasted every social convention out of his head.

"What? Is something wrong?" Eyes wide, Matty stared at him.

He shook his head, still unable to formulate words with his libido zinging into overdrive.

"Does this look all right?" She dipped her chin toward her chest.

Matty wore a skintight, leather jump suit that stretched over a perfectly flat stomach down into a magnetizing vee atop slim, toned legs. The leather caressed her full breasts and made his hands itch to caress them, too. Thigh-high, black-studded boots seemed glued to her legs. Tiny black ears stuck out of her caramel curled hair. A cat mask around those smoky chocolate, feline eyes completed the outfit.

"I'm Cat Woman from the *Batman* movie. Say something."

"I can't speak." He took a deep gulp of wine. "You look amazing. And this is something you just happened to have in your closet?"

No flippant answer, just a Cheshire grin. *Lady, this is going to be some date.*

"What do you think of the wine? I can bring a couple of bottles to Kay's if you like it."

"You'll be the hit of the party. The Sullivan women can put away the wine."

"Great. I have a few bottles left. I found this great winery when I was in California. It's called Longboard. I met the winemaker who is the most charismatic man and I've been drinking their wine exclusively ever since. Let me grab the bottles. I don't think I need a jacket. Aren't we lucky that it is such a warm day? I remember last year it snowed on Halloween."

"I wish I could forget that snow. We froze last year. It was a luau theme. Leis and little else."

Hooking her hand in the crook of his arm, the benign wizard, Harry, escorted whip-toting Cat Woman to the car.

****

Speechless at the spectacle in the wealthy suburban neighborhood of mini-mansions, Matilda peered out the windows as Brian turned into a cul-de-sac. A huge tent covered the front yard sheltering a milling throng. Children in costumes scooted to and from the stately colonial house.

"There must be a hundred people here," she commented, amazed.

"More people come each year. Half the precinct brings their kids and some of Mike's staff from the hospital brings their kids. Fun, huh?"

"I'll bet." Cocooned in the car, observing the antics of the crowd was pure entertainment. "It's a circus."

"No, that was the theme two years ago." Brian chortled, jumped out of the jeep, hurried around the hood and opened the door for her.

Grabbing the bottles of wine from the back seat she handed them out to Brian who tucked one under his arm, held one in hand and extended a free hand down to her. Taking his outstretched hand had the same electric effect on her as the symbolic little bolt on his forehead, reverberating beneath every inch of her leather-encased body. With a shudder and an intake of breath she planted her spiked boots on pavement and left the car.

"Uncle Brian!"

"Uncle Brian!"

Two tow-headed children hurled themselves down the lawn towards Brian. He handed the two wine bottles over to Matilda, bent to scoop the kids up in each arm and twirled them around.

"Hey, squirts." He carefully placed them back on the lawn. The identical girls dressed as Dalmatian puppies wiggled and grabbed each of his hands towing him towards the tent.

"Whoa, wait a minute, pups. We can't leave Cat Woman behind." Tugging the kids to a standstill, he stooped down to their eye level.

Encircling them with his arms, he looked at each child then up at Matilda. "Say hi to Aunt Matty."

Her heart rolled. *Aunt Matty. He's making me part of his family.* Deeply complimented, unbridled pleasure warred with her usual self-imposed constraints. *Is this happening too fast? Am I ready to plunge into his world, make it mine? I want to move forward. I want him.*

"Hello, Aunt Matty." The identical little girls chorused.

"I'm Peggy."

"And I'm Amanda." The introductions came in indistinguishable pitches.

"Hi, Peggy and Amanda. I'm very happy to meet you." Instantly Matilda fell in love with the pair.

"We are Uncle Brian's favorite nieces." Peggy gazed adoringly at Brian.

"But it's a secret." Amanda added, holding a pudgy finger to her lips. "You can't tell anyone."

"I promise I won't tell." Matilda mimicked Amanda's shushing gesture.

"Come on, Uncle Brian. Daddy's doing bobbing for apples."

"You go ahead and we'll catch up in a few minutes. I want to say hi to your mommy first."

"OK." The girls raced back towards the tent.

"Thank you." Matilda linked her arm through his, a lovely surge of possessiveness.

"For what?"

"For making me feel like a part of your family."

Brian laughed as a red-haired pirate holding a wailing baby headed in their direction. "Don't thank me before you get to know them."

"I am so done with this. See if you can make him

stop crying. Danny dumped him on me. Take a turn." The pirate unceremoniously transferred the squawking baby with a runny nose into Brian's arms.

"Is ugly old Uncle Patrick making you cry, Joey?" Brian asked the now hiccupping child, a smug expression aimed at Patrick the Pirate, hardly ugly or old, an attractive smattering of faint freckles over his nose and cheeks, boyish rather than equipped to plunder and loot.

Patrick ignored him and turned his attention toward Matty. "Wine, great. Let's find some glasses." He snatched the bottles of wine away from her with a devilish grin, clasped her hand and pulled her towards the front door.

Brian caught up and walked by her side, quieting the blotchy-faced baby as he bounced him on his hip. Patrick held the door open allowing Matilda and Brian to pass through and then followed to the kitchen in the back of the house where Cruella de Ville took a tray of cookies out of the oven.

The heavenly smell of chocolate filled the air making Matilda's stomach grumble.

"Hi. Great costume." Cruella set the tray on the grates of the gargantuan industrial stove.

"Thanks, sis. Do you think Mary will remember the hours I spent reading Harry Potter books to her?"

"I'm sure she will, Bri, but I wasn't talking to you. I was referring to your costume, Cat Woman."

"Thank you." Matilda hugged her on impulse and was pleased with the returned squeeze. "I'm sure you don't remember me. Kay, right?"

Cruella nodded, smiling.

"I'm Matty Connors. Gosh those cookies smell delicious."

"I do remember meeting you at the hospital. Nice to see you again. Help yourself before the vultures smell them and they vanish." Kay snorted.

"Of course we all remember you." Patrick grabbed a cookie, blew on it, tossing it from hand to hand, and then popped the whole thing in his mouth. "You're Brian's date from the wedding. He had to hit you over the head to go out with him."

"You're a real comedian, Pat." Brian hoisted the baby over to his brother. "Go find Danny and tell him I think Joey here is hungry. And changing his diaper would be a good idea, too."

"Save some wine for me." Patrick went in search of his brother.

"Please sit down, Matty and make yourself comfortable." Kay wielded a spatula, efficiently transferring the cookies from the baking sheet to a plate. "Brian how about opening that wine for us?" Kay brought the heaping plate and three glasses over to the table in two trips.

"This is an amazing party. I have never seen anything like it." Matilda took a bite of a warm, gooey cookie and sighed at the sensual pleasure of dark chocolate melting in her mouth. "These are wonderful."

"Enjoy. Our Halloween party guest list mushrooms more each year. I almost cancelled this year. It's just not the same without Jimmy." Kay's eyes clouded and Matty nodded, understanding.

"But everyone looks forward to it. I probably look forward to it the most. It's not easy to come up with original themes each year. Any suggestions next year would be greatly appreciated."

Next year. Will there be next year for me with Brian? Please God, yes.

The back door opened and Fred Flintstone wearing sort of a slingshot over his eye stomped into the kitchen.

"Hey, Fred."

"Hey, Harry."

"Where's Wilma and Pebbles."

"Following right behind. Kay, can I put this formula in the fridge?"

"Sure, Joe, if you can find room."

He inserted bottles here and there on the crowded shelf then grabbed a cookie and stuffed it in his mouth.

Matilda sipped wine and gazed out the kitchen window, spying Wilma carrying tiny baby Pebbles, an elastic headband with the requisite attached bone atop a cap of wispy strawberry hair. Scarlet O'Hara and Rhett Butler followed behind holding hands and laughing.

"That's Bobbie with Emma Jean and Molly and Danny are gone with the wind. Nutty family, huh?" Brian surrounded her with warmth, his chest pressed against her back, his chin rested on the crown of her head. Shielded with his arms wrapped around her waist, she leaned against him, protected, belonging right there.

Turning her face up towards his, she smiled into his twinkling blue-green eyes. "I feel a little like Alice in Wonderland."

The wine circulated and laughter and love filled the kitchen.

Later pressed into the games by pint-sized manipulators, Matilda bobbed for apples, played pin the horn on Shrek, burped babies and read spooky Halloween storybooks aloud, loving every minute of it. When even the sugar high couldn't keep the little ones awake the party ended. Matilda and Brian were the last to leave after they helped Kay and Mike clean up.

Brian draped his arm around her shoulders as they strolled back to the jeep.

"Thank you for bringing me, Brian. I had a wonderful time."

"I'm glad." Brian adjusted the heat, a welcome blast out of the vents in the now sunless autumn chill. "I had a good time, too."

Driving back to her house classical music on the radio and the interruptions of the velvety-voiced announcer occasionally broke the comfortable silence between them.

All her well-honed instincts in play, Matilda didn't hesitate to extend the fun day she'd had with Brian. "Want to come in for a little while?" She faced him as he pulled up to the curb in front of her house.

"That would be nice." He put his finger under her chin and leaned in for a light peck on her lips before turning off the ignition. She waited in the warm seat for him to open her door, anticipating the next kiss. *I'm not going to over-think this. I'll know if I'm ready.*

Brian plucked her house keys out of her hand and opened the door for her. As soon as he shoved the door closed with the click of the latch, he took her in his arms and kissed her deeply. Breathless, she returned the passion, melting by degrees.

Still clasping her against his chest he ended the kiss and searched her eyes. A thrill ricocheted inside her at the naked desire she detected in his eyes and in his throaty inflection, "I have been waiting all night to do this."

His fingers clasped the zipper on the front of her jumpsuit and inched it down, his eyes locked on hers. His other hand blazed a trail against her skin following the path exposed by the gaping material.

"Your skin is like satin." He bowed his head and kissed bare skin, a riot of scorching tremors with each brush of his lips. "Even softer than I dreamed." Head bent, lips against her cleavage, he pressed her closer.

Her fingers threaded lightly through the soft, thick hair at the nape of his neck. "Brian," she whispered.

As he raised his head, she cupped the edges of his jaws and lifted his face toward her parted lips. He took them fiercely, his beard stubble abrading her skin, the sweet taste of his tongue a heady, thrilling pleasure that stoked pulsing need in her core.

He lifted his head and smiled, his eyes glazed with desire.

Dazed in the wake of the delicious kiss, she didn't impede him when he slowly zipped the jumpsuit back up, his eyes never leaving hers.

Clearing his throat first, he uttered, "I better leave now."

"All right." She nodded. "Yes, I think that's best."

"Thank you for a fantastic first date. I hope we can do this again soon."

"I'd like that *very* much."

"Great. I'll call you." He kissed her deeply one more time, opened the door and left her dreamy, spinning.

Leaning her cheek against the doorframe's cool wood, she followed him down the front steps, around the car, into the street with her eyes. With the long robe concealing the muscular lines of him, he looked a bit Harry-Potterish. Still quaking from his far from boyish good night kisses, Cat Woman returned Harry's wave and closed the door.

Hey. Thanks. It shouldn't have come to this, you know? Hell, it's only money. I'm sorry I pressed so hard. But man, a shot in the leg is nothing if I don't settle this score. But, hey, I'm bleeding here. Just help me now, all right?

Chapter 8

Matilda pinched the sides of her forehead with a thumb and pinky, concentrating on Jake's message with all her senses, but nothing more came. *A shot in the leg over money. Ben came back to help you?* Didn't jibe with the conclusion that Ben shot *and* killed Jake and certainly clouded the order of events in the case. She kneaded her temples remembering her recent call to Lexxie Ashford-Whitman. The terrified mother didn't want to accept the truth that Matilda had reported, but the woman trusted her and probably knew in her heart all along that her son was dead. Matilda had advised Lexxie she'd no longer consult with her on the case but the police would aggressively pursue suspects and search for Jake's body. Not the whole truth, but better this way for Matilda.

Also better not to discuss this latest truth with Brian. She'd be on shaky grounds convincing him not to waver on her conviction that Jake was dead and not re-classify the case as a missing person's investigation.

Rising from behind her desk she wandered to the window, stretched two slats of the blinds open wider and peered through the gap at the parking area of the clinic. Her office door opened behind her, a whine and squeal of hinges.

"Want me to pick up some lunch for you?" Shamus asked. "I'm heading to Panera."

"No, that's OK," she replied, pivoting to face him. "I'm not hungry and I only have ten minutes before my next appointment."

Doing a double take, Shamus scrutinized her.

"You feeling all right? You can eat more than me. Sit."

Matilda sat, not at all irritated by her brother's gruff command. Anyone who didn't know him would probably be intimidated by Shamus. The man didn't speak. He growled, rumbled, almost roared. Built like an O-lineman with brown hair curling over his ears and a scruffy beard, Shamus cut an imposing figure. Same for Brian who was about the same height as Shamus. She smiled at the mental image of Brian and Shamus side by side—leopard versus bear.

Shamus stuffed himself in her antique rocker, his hands folded across his middle, creaking the chair ominously. Matilda always feared that the man would turn it into splinters.

"Now, Matty girl. What's taken your appetite away and put that faraway look on your face?" He always employed Grandma Pearl's brogue when a lecture was imminent.

Grinning, she replied, "A man."

That stopped the rocking.

"Well, well. When do I get to meet him?" His blue eyes twinkled as he brushed a huge paw over his beard.

"You already have." Resting an elbow on her desk, she propped her chin on her hand.

He scrunched up his face. "I must be daft. I don't remember a gentleman caller."

"At the hospital. The man in the tuxedo. I hit his car."

Shamus dropped his eyes downward, a thoughtful expression. "Which man in a tuxedo? There was a bunch of them."

There sure was. Chuckling, she was more specific, "He was the one who insisted I get my cut looked at by a doctor. His name is Brian Sullivan."

Shamus resumed rocking. "Seemed like a nice enough guy. Good Irish name. And I like his concern for your welfare. So?" His eyes squinted, lips stretched in an ear-to-ear grin, her loving inquisitor.

"He took me to a costume party at his sister's house on Halloween. We had a blast."

"Aha." Eyebrows dipping, his face turned serious. "Today's All Souls Day. How come you're not in California at the cemetery?"

Matilda chewed the corner of her lip. "I cancelled the reservation." The warmth in Shamus' eyes encouraged her. "For a lot of reasons. I don't need to go there to remember Eric. I'll never forget him, but I'm ready to live without him now."

"And this Brian Sullivan prompted your decision?"

She straightened in the seat. "Yes. Yes he did."

Flexing his biceps, Shamus exerted enough pressure on the armrests of the rocker to extract himself and then approached her desk. He grasped her hand. "Good. I'm glad for you, Matty." His beard tickled as he pecked her on the cheek. "But I need to meet the man before I give you big brother approval. What does he do?"

"He's a homicide detective. I'm working with him on a case."

Eyes widened with alarm Shamus exclaimed, "Now you're the daft one!"

She patted his hand. "It's OK, I can handle it. I never told you the details about what happened to Eric…"

"You didn't have to," he growled. Pacing in front of her desk he continued, "I was the one who came running in the middle of the night because of your screams. I held you while you shook like you had been electrocuted, both of us drenched with sweat. I never wanted the details and I don't want them now."

Head bent, she nodded all the while he ranted. She remembered. Vividly. "I exposed Eric to danger with my involvement with that case," Matilda admitted. "But Brian is a trained professional. This is different."

Shamus might be intimidating, but he truly loved her, had her best interests at heart. "OK, OK," he said more reasonably, a rumble instead of a growl. "You know?" Shamus grinned at her, boyish. "I used to be jealous that you had the gift and I didn't."

"Ha. You had every reason." Matilda poised her finger over the intercom button on her phone when it buzzed. "I always knew where you hid your Halloween candy."

"You little brat." Shamus shook his head.

The buzzer rasped again and Matilda tapped the button. "Yes, Trudy?"

"You have Mitzy the Maltese in room two," the receptionist announced.

"Gotcha." Matilda shoved her chair back and skirted the desk as Shamus rose, capturing her in a bear hug.

He held her at arms length. "Maybe you can set a date with your cop to go out with Cara and me sometime?"

Matilda beamed, liking the sound of "your cop." "Sounds great. I'll invite him."

Light on her feet, Matilda scurried through the hall toward the exam room, steering to the open door where she observed her patient trotting around the legs of his toddler master, Jack. His mom watched from a corner stool. Jack wore adorable denim jeans and a long sleeve, silk-screened shirt—a cobalt blue Little Engine That Could on steeply inclined tracks.

A handgun in a boxcar.

Matilda backed away from the open door, leaned her back against the wall, eyes closed. *The gun in the train car, barely large enough to contain it. Wood. Paneling? A crate? Dim brownish light.* Opening her eyes, the image of the handgun in the boxcar remained intact. *It's there all right. But where is there?*

Matilda resolved to call Brian after she treated Mitzy.

Fifteen minutes later she dialed his number, excited to impart the sketchy information but anxious about how he'd receive it.

"Hello, my lady," Brian answered. A shimmer of delight at the possessive reference emboldened Matilda.

"Hey, my cop," she countered. "I have a bit of possibly useless information." Sucking in a breath she reported, "My sense is I saw the gun Ben used to shoot Jake, but I'm not positive. In a boxcar. Small. Must be a train set. But a rather large—"

"Holy shit!" Brian exclaimed. Her mouth fell open. "I'm on my way over. Can you break away?"

"Sure..." Leafing through her appointment calendar, she checked her patient load. "I don't have anything until three. Will that give us enough time?"

"It should. I'll round up Joe. You might be able to help pinpoint where to look in the trailer," Brian fired the statements at her, obviously charged up. "I sure hope he didn't ditch it when they moved."

"Where are we going? I have no clue where this box car is located."

"I do," Brian sang out. "It's in a mobile home park near O'Hare. If he moved the train set with him. When we searched Ben's trailer after Jake was reported missing, I saw an elaborate train set in a storage closet. I'm on my way. Lady, I could kiss you!"

Her lips curled in a smile, thrilled with his reaction. "I'll meet you out front."

Matilda hung up, her pulse racing and tugged absently on a tendril of hair escaped from her ponytail. How exhilarating to use her gift again to help find Jake's killer. Even more special, she'd help the police succeed. This time not just for the rewards that came from seeing justice served through the hard work of law enforcers she respected. This time, she cared deeply about the law enforcer.

Maybe I should go fix my hair.

****

I must be screwy to get excited about this. But it has to be legit. How could she know about the giant train set in Ben's closet?

"You bring that copy of the original search warrant?" Joe's deep voice cut through.

Brian patted his chest. "In my pocket. We won't need it, though. Ben knows the drill from the first time."

"Is it still enforceable?"

"Caprisi's taking care of the technicalities just in case. Same residence, but since it's a mobile home he's covering our bases with the new address. "Brian glanced sideways to observe Joe nodding. "We can take anything material we find."

"Good work."

Joe's acknowledgment meant a lot.

Branches swished scratchy against the sides of the jeep as it slowly rolled clear of the tree line into the parking apron in front of the animal clinic. The car bounced as it hit a rut, prompting Brian's mental note to get the bumper fixed. The bungee cord wouldn't hold much longer.

"Now isn't that a pretty sight?" Joe tilted his head, peering at Brian over the rim of his sunglasses, and then he faced forward presumably to catch the pretty sight again.

Matty stood a few feet ahead at the base of the clinic steps, sunshine highlighting her mane of gleaming, honey blonde hair, slouchy bag hung over her shoulder, her quilted car coat obscuring the lush curves that had Brian horny since he had unzipped her cat woman costume. *Matty is a very pretty sight in or out of that boxy coat. Preferably out.*

Brian braked amid a racket of stirred up gravel, and rolled down the window. "Hop in."

"If you don't mind, I'll follow you in my car? Just in case it takes longer than expected."

"No problem." Brian swung his left arm out the window and caught up her hand on the fly. Spontaneously he swept her palm toward his lips and kissed a spot dead center, her fresh citrus scent and silky skin a pleasure worth the faint whistle his brother emitted that surely would involve razzing the entire car ride to the Jarvis trailer.

Matty graced Brian with a sweet smile when he let her have her hand back and ducked around the hood of the jeep toward the back of the building. An engine turned over and rolling gravel preceded the appearance of her car, now idling as Brian executed a three-point turn and headed back out to the street, Matty following.

"You have something going with Matty Connors?" Joe asked, subtlety dependably lacking when Sullivan boys interacted with each other.

"Yeah. Something," Brian tossed out, applying the brake as he neared the yellow light. *And there'll be more something if she's free for dinner tonight.*

"Do you think that's smart?" Joe persisted. "The case and all?"

Coming to a full stop at the light, Brian turned toward Joe who trained his intractable blue eye on him.

"You of all people have something against socializing on the job?" Brian grinned. "The old ball and chain chafing with former agent Bobbie Leighton?"

Joe snorted. "Hell, no. I'm talking about Matty Connors, bro. You think you can handle a woman like her?"

It was Brian's turn to snort. "Hell, yes. But I haven't gotten to the point of *handling* her yet."

Brian navigated up the ramp and gunned the engine to merge with highway traffic, glancing in the rearview window to make sure Matty was still keeping up with him. Satisfied when she followed, Brian sped up.

"Good for you," Joe commented. "I think it would be hard to be with a woman who's...all knowing. Mysterious."

Brian laughed. "Look, Joe. I have no clue what all these supposed visions are about. Frankly, I find it hard to take them seriously."

"Sure you do," Joe sneered. "That's why we're scrambling to a trailer park to seize a murder weapon she saw in a little train."

You've got a point. "You're the one who insisted we take her seriously, so I'm following orders." Brian checked her progress in the mirror again. "Anyway. Aren't all women all knowing?"

Joe grunted. "Hell, yeah. Bobbie knows what I'm thinking before I think it."

****

The mobile home park was deserted, a forlorn scraggly plot of earth dotted with a collection of residences more like a used car lot laden with dents and rust spots with a few tattered awnings flapping over tin doors. Pulling up in front of Ben's trailer, Brian cut the engine, slid out of the jeep and waited at the side of his car for Matty to park behind him.

He ambled over to the driver window. "Anything?" Brian asked her when the window slid down.

She furrowed her brow, confusion swimming in her soft, hypnotic brown eyes. "Pardon me?"

"Is this the place?" Brian pressed her, keeping his mind on the murder weapon instead of thinking about how much he wanted to handle Matty Connors.

"Oh." She wagged her head around, peering through the windshield. "I have no idea. Do you want me to go in with you?"

"Yes." Brian pulled on the door handle and swung it open. "Please."

At the door, Joe pounded a dull, tinny drumbeat. "Police. Please open the door."

On creaking hinges the door swung forward revealing Ben in the doorway, his features shadowed in the dim interior light. "What the hell do you want now?"

"We'd like to look around inside. Can we come in?" Brian asked pleasantly.

"Do I have a choice?" Ben's feet were planted on either side of the frame, his legs forming a V over a ragged throw rug.

"Not really," Brian replied, still pleasant, already advancing toward Ben. Joe followed and Brian stepped aside allowing Joe and Matty to enter the limited space.

Matty drew near, touched the cuff of Brian's shirt and whispered, "This is it. Where Jake was shot."

Brian nodded, cupped her hand with his.

"Who's she?" Ben demanded. "Why do I have to let her in here?"

"*She* is Matilda Connors and she's here because I say so." Brian stared the kid down, noted the beads of sweat gathering on his upper lip and forehead.

"Have a seat over there while my colleagues have a look around," Joe asserted, waving a hand toward a table and a couple chairs.

Ben limped the few feet to the table and plunked into a seat. Brian motioned for Matty to follow him down the skinny hallway toward the closet he remembered. Every minute detail of the original search was emblazoned in Brian's memory and nothing looked different in the sorry, smelly place.

As he hoped, the large mildewed cardboard box was still in the closet. Squatting, Brian heaved the box toward him. Matty leaned over his shoulder as he spread the flaps open. "Here you go, lady. A train set."

Her warm hands rested on his shoulders,

infusing him with all sorts of anticipation. Methodically he removed train cars from the box, hoisting the boxcar straight up, victorious and then, down, discouraged. Too light. Setting it on the stained linoleum floor, he slid the miniature side door of the car open. Stuck his hand inside, a snug fit. Nothing. Shook it for good measure before he handed it to her over his shoulder without looking back at her.

"This isn't the one." Her sweet voice did nothing to diminish his disappointment.

Tilting the empty cardboard box as he leaned back on his heels he spit out, "Obviously."

"Brian..."

Sweeping the train cars into the circle of his arms, he scooped them up and dumped them back in the box with a couple of aggravated, aggressive motions. Brian straightened his legs to stand and shoved the box back into the closet with a toe of his boot before he turned to face Matty.

Her crestfallen expression should have tempered his reaction, but Brian was beyond frustrated with her whimsical *truths*. He had gone to Caprisi with this and couldn't bear to face the man empty-handed. His reputation was at stake and he couldn't believe he had entrusted it to a psychic. "Thanks for nothing," he stated in a cold monotone.

"I just *told* you, Brian, this isn't the one I saw. It was blue, with white letters on one side. It had two larger letters, like a logo, on the other side. A "B" and an "M"—"

Brian cut her off. "Right. When we come across a blue train, I'm sure there'll be a gun inside."

Those chocolate eyes held no softness now squinted into slits, her lips tensed in a thin line. Brian preferred she'd keep them clamped shut like that, but no. "Brian, I know what I saw. The gun is in a boxcar." She heaved a breath. "Somewhere!"

"Everything OK back there?" Joe yelled.

Brian dragged a hand through his hair as Matty steamed past him down the hall and out the door of the trailer with a clang. Ambling toward Joe, Brian quipped, "Yeah, everything's great."

Joe cast him a questioning eye and Brian flicked his eyes toward the door as he moved in that direction. "We're done here."

Standing on the threadbare throw rug in front of the door waiting for Joe to join him, Brian glanced down. The rug wasn't included in the catalog of meager belongings in the trailer Brian had memorized. Couldn't have been purchased in the six months since the original search of the premises. Had to be years old. Despite the lack of any apparent housekeeping skills even Ben and his roommate, Jodi, couldn't have worn it down this much.

Joe shuffled next to him, but Brian didn't raise his head, fixated on various sized blotches of discolorations on the woven material. Looked scrubbed, maybe bleached. Brian raised his head and trained his eyes on Ben Jarvis, sweating profusely, and it clicked. *Tried to remove the bloodstains, did you, Ben?*

Off the rug in one stride, Brian squatted down and rolled it up with four twists. "Yep, we're done here, soon as we give you a receipt for this fine welcome mat of yours."

Chapter 9

Jodi Wilson twisted to peer over her shoulder, rushing, pushing toward the house, fear stiffening her muscles. *Just let me get there. Please God, let me get home.* Her heart pounded against her rib cage as she increased the pace, legs pumping, shoes thudding against the concrete. Her heavy book bag slammed against her hip as she turned a corner. Leaves skittered across the sidewalk in front of her. Again she looked over her shoulder. *I know someone's there.*

"Ben, is that you?" No answer. "Ben, I swear if you think this is funny I will kill you." Again, no answer. Faint footsteps shuffled behind her, but when she turned to confront Ben or whoever, she saw no one. *Ben would never do this to me.* Panic gripped her. Ever since Jake disappeared that terrifying night, too many questions hung unanswered and fear stalked her.

Gasping for air she bounded up the brick stairs, her hand grasping the iron railing. The keys slipped through her shaking fingers twice before she was able to fit the key in the lock and slam the door behind her. A quick flip of a switch on the wall and bright lights flooded the first floor of the townhouse. She leaned her back against the door, breathing hard.

"Mom. Mom!" Only silence. Her heart lurched. Her mother hadn't returned home from work yet and she was alone in the house.

Tears rolled down her cheeks. Her entire body trembled as she slid downward, her back against the door and landed on the area rug with a thump. She dug a hand in her bag and rummaged around the bottom for her cell phone. Heavy footsteps thudded on the steps outside, followed by a loud knock on the door that rattled through her. She shoved away from the door as if scalded, her rear end sliding along the floor. The doorbell chimes echoed through the house.

"Jodi? It's me. Are you there? I thought I saw you on the street," his deep voice boomed, familiar.

Relief flooded through her as she recognized the voice on the other side of the door. *Thank God.* She jumped up forgetting the phone, slid the chain into the slot and opened the door a crack.

"Hi. Did you see anyone skulking around out there?" Her voice pitched high, shaky.

"No. Why? Is everything all right?" He knit his brows, a kind expression on his face.

"I think someone was following me. Gave me the creeps." She heaved a sigh, smelled damp wood with her face so close to the edge of the door.

"I didn't see anyone. Why would anyone be following you?"

"I don't know. Maybe something to do with Jake..." Closing her eyes she willed her pulse rate to slow down. Glancing at him again, he smiled, reassuring and she managed a weak smile in return. "What are you doing here?"

"Can I come in?" His smile widened.

"Sorry." Jodi shook her head embarrassed at her rude treatment of him while she unhooked the chain and swung the door open. "Sure. Come on in."

He crossed the threshold and stood politely aside while she closed the door. "You're very pale. Can I get you a drink of water or something?" He touched her jacket sleeve, his gloved fingers warm against her forearm, further reassuring her.

"I was so scared, but I'm OK now. Thanks anyway." She grinned up at him.

"Did you call the police and tell them someone was following you?"

Shaking her head, steady on her feet now, maybe she had imagined the whole thing. "No. I was about to, but then you rang the bell. I'm fine now with you here."

He drew a gun out of his coat pocket and pointed it at her.

"Are you sure?"

****

The curtain moved, fell back in place and the door opened before Brian had a chance to ring the bell.

Bobbie held an index finger against her lips shushing him. "Joe almost has Emma asleep," she whispered, holding the door open for him.

Inside Brian accompanied her to the kitchen in the back of the house.

"The place looks great." Brian commented, assessing the transformation since he and the rest of his brothers had helped move Joe and Bobbie in their new home.

"It's getting there. Not enough time in the day to get everything organized. Little by little, it's coming together. What's in the bags?" Bobbie eyed the stuff Brian deposited on the kitchen table.

"I picked up some wings, beer and a bottle of that wine you liked so much at the Halloween party." Brian unpacked the bags, left the lid on the container of wings to keep them hot.

Bobbie reached into the cabinet over the sink, grabbed three wine glasses and set them on the counter. Pulling open a drawer near the sink, she picked up a corkscrew and tossed it to him. "Let's open up that wine."

Brian caught it in one hand, used it on the bottle. "Rough day?"

"Not really. Just long..." Bobbie pulled out a chair, accepted the glass of wine he handed her. "Emma's a little cranky, but I wouldn't change one second of my life."

Brian popped the top off a bottle of beer with his thumb, took a deep slug and then sat across from her at the table.

Sipping her wine, her amber eyes peered over the rim of the glass, dancing with amusement. Swallowing, she sighed, contented, and set the wine glass down on the table. "Speaking of the Halloween party..."

"Were we?"

"Yes, we were. It was great spending time with your lady, Matty. She's great."

The Sullivan women are unapologetically nosy. "Yeah, great."

"What's up? Trouble?" Bobbie fingered the stem of the wine glass.

"Not really. This is all so frustrating. I start to believe in all this psychic mumbo jumbo and it backfires on me. I guess Joe told you she led us on a wild goose chase."

Joe strode into the kitchen his face lit up with a wide grin. He rested his hands on Bobbie's shoulders, beaming at Brian. "Success. The princess is asleep."

Bobbie cupped a hand over Joe's and arched her neck to gaze up at him. "Thank you, honey."

"My pleasure. What were you talking about?"

"Nothing," Brian responded, grabbing a beer and offering it to Joe.

"Matty," Bobbie contradicted Brian.

"I didn't have a chance to tell you, Bobbie." Joe accepted the beer, sat at the table. "Matty saw," Joe made quotes in the air, "a gun in a train set. Ben has trains. We thought we had him, but we didn't find the gun. Brian's steamed about it."

Bobbie nodded her head at Brian's scowl.

Joe popped the beer open, drank down a couple gulps. "Something will come of it. Cut Matty a break. I'm telling you she's never wrong."

"First time for everything," Brian countered.

Good thing Forensics has that rug to work on. "We did confiscate possible evidence so maybe her lead wasn't a total loss. Blood stains are visible on a small rug we took from the trailer. Lab's working on it now."

"Enough work for tonight." Bobbie skewered first Joe, then Brian, with a pointed look. "Emma has been up all day. Let's enjoy the peace and quiet while we can." She took another sip of wine, "Ah. This wine's wonderful. You men hungry?"

"Duh." Brian grinned at her.

"Good. Help me get dinner on the table, sweetie?"

Joe carried a pot of bubbling chili to the table while Bobbie brought bowls of cheese, tomatoes, lettuce and sour cream. Brian opened the Styrofoam container and piled steaming wings on a plate setting it down next to the pot of chili.

"This smells great. Thanks, sis. I'm starving."

For a comfortable few minutes, spoons scraped against bowls.

"Delicious." Joe sat back in his seat and patted his flat stomach. Bobbie stood to clear the table.

"Sit down, sis. I'll take care of the dishes. It's the least I can do after such a great dinner."

Bobbie deferred to Brian at the sink, sat at the table and put her feet in Joe's lap. "You are the best, Brian. Thank you. Are you staying for the football game?"

"If it's OK with you guys." Brian sunk his arms up to his elbows in warm sudsy water.

"Sure, of course we might be asleep before halftime."

Brian rinsed dishes, loaded the dishwasher, scrubbed the pot and wiped the placemats off before stowing them in the closet where they belonged, according to his brother.

Bobbie left the men and went upstairs to check on Emma when cooing noises sounded over the baby monitor. Joe's face transformed, tender, ecstatic as he leaned closer to the device while Bobbie sang a lullaby and Emma garbled sweetly.

"You're a lucky man, bro." Brian finished the kitchen work and sat across the table from Joe, the dish towel thrown casually over his shoulder.

"I thank God everyday for my two ladies." Joe's eye glistened.

Envy pinched Brian witnessing his brother's outpouring, an unexpected emotion. Joe had found everything he wanted in Bobbie. Brian couldn't deny sensing something similar with Matty. More and more something was missing for Brian that had nothing to do with Jake Ashford's case.

Bobbie waltzed into the kitchen, humming, Emma cradled near her breast, the baby's eyes wide with delight gazing up at her mother.

"Uncle Brian, do you want to hold the princess while I warm her bottle?"

"I would love to." With Emma, a warm delicate bundle nestled safely in the crook of his arm, Brian went into the living room and sat in the red corduroy rocker in front of the flat screen TV. Crystal blue eyes stared at him, wide, innocent, perhaps not fully focused on the toothy grin he gave back to her. His heart melted. She grasped his finger and stuck the tip of it in her rose bud mouth after a few attempts, her lips smacking as she gummed it, sucked with little tugs.

He wanted this. He wanted to hold his child. His child and Matty's. Shaken by the unaccustomed raw emotions, he was relieved to hand Emma back to her mom. Bobbie sat next to Joe on the sofa. *I want what Joe has, a wife he adores and a child to spoil.* What he lacked he had unconsciously known he had found the moment he set eyes on Matilda Connors.

The cell phone on Brian's belt vibrated. Brian plucked it out of the holder, flipped it open and answered. "Yeah. OK. I copy. Thanks, Nagle."

"What's up?" Joe asked as Brian stood.

"An anonymous call just came through. Gunshots fired on Canterbury Lane."

"That's only a couple of blocks away. Why'd he call you? You aren't covering tonight, are you?"

"Nope, but he recognized the name from the Ashford case. It's Jodi Wilson's house."

"Let me grab my coat. I'll ride with you." Joe leaned over, kissed Bobbie and kissed the top of Emma's head.

"I'll try to be back soon."

"No problem. Just be safe."

"Sorry to dine and dash, sis."

"Come back again soon."

"Thanks, I will."

Outside, Brian and Joe sprinted down the front walk to Brian's jeep.

"Take a left at the corner. Canterbury is about six blocks over." Joe fastened his seat belt as Brian accelerated away from the curb and left the bumper behind in front of Bobbie and Joe's. Bringing the jeep to a screeching stop at the corner, a squad car, lights flashing, sped past them through the intersection.

"Good, Morales and Conklin are responding." Brian turned onto the street and tailed them. The squad car's headlights fanned across the lawn of the corner house as it turned onto Canterbury, Brian's jeep close behind.

"Bri. Did you see that?" Joe leaned forward, peering through the windshield.

"Yeah. Someone cut across the lawn."

Brian yanked the wheel, pulled the jeep over to the curb and jumped out of the car. He raced across the lawn with Joe's pounding feet close behind. Breathing hard, Brian took a leap at the shadowy form sprinting ahead of him and made a flying tackle.

"What the hell, man. I didn't do anything."

Brian recognized the muffled voice underneath him.

Pushing up into a crouch over Ben Jarvis' body, Brian pinned his arms back at the wrists. "Well, well, what have we here? Joe why do you think our buddy Ben is running across lawns at night?"

"Can't say."

Brian glared into Ben's eyes. "Why were you running?"

"Since when is it illegal to jog, man?" Sweat poured down Ben's face, trickled into an eye. He squinted the eye, blinked a couple times.

"In the dark and through peoples' yards? Hmm. Let me think if I buy that. While I'm thinking, Joe, read him his rights."

"You have the right to remain silent. Anything you say can and will be used against you in a court of law." Joe snapped handcuffs on Ben and Brian turned him and pulled him to his feet. "You have the right to have an attorney present during questioning. If you cannot afford an attorney, one will be appointed for you. Do you understand these rights?"

Ben remained silent. Brian pulled on his cuffs.

"Do you understand?"

"Yeah, I understand. I didn't do anything to her." Tears welled in Ben's eyes. "I—"

"Her? Who's *her*?" Brian demanded.

Ben hung his head, mute.

Brian tugged Ben forward towards the jeep. The scanner on the dashboard crackled as Joe stuffed Ben into the back seat and then jumped in the front seat next to Brian.

"Where are you taking me? I want a lawyer."

Ignoring him, Brian drove the jeep down the street and pulled behind the squad car. Morales stood next to the car talking on his phone. Conklin wrapped bright, yellow police tape around the trees in front of a row of townhouses to keep the neighbors and curious back from the crime scene.

"Hey." Morales snapped his phone closed and ambled over to Brian and Joe as they stepped out of the jeep.

"Hey, Morales. What you got?"

"Female, eighteen to twenty-five years old, shot once in the head, gun dropped next to the body. Secured the scene, medical examiner on the way."

"Identification?" Brian asked.

"Not yet.

A woman clad in a waitress uniform tore down the street toward Brian. Conklin dropped the tape and grabbed her arm to prevent her from running up the walkway toward the Wilson house.

"This is my house. Is my daughter OK?" She stared at her wide open front door and then back at Conklin. "Jodi! Jodi! No, no!" she screamed.

****

Brian slammed his desk drawer, furious that he hadn't pressured a confession out of Ben before he had lawyered up.

"Easy, Bri." Joe shook his head. "Nothing we can do about it. We don't have enough to charge him. He's in a cell downstairs. Caught running near the scene, fingerprints on file. If he's the perp we don't have to go far to wrap this up."

"Damn it, Joe. I know he killed Jodi Wilson and I'd bet Jake Ashford, too. My guess is she knew what he did to Jake. He had to silence her."

"We'll nail him. We should have the medical examiner's report in a few days. Now we have a gun. If there is any evidence connecting Ben, we'll nail him. Come on. Call it a night. Let's go watch the rest of the game."

"Nah. I'll just finish the paperwork and head on home."

"OK. See you tomorrow."

Brian dealt with the paperwork in the quiet squad room, reluctant to go home. Watching Jodi's mother collapse on the porch at the sight of her daughter's lifeless body drove home the shortness of life. He wanted more in his life than casual friendly relationships. A wife and family waiting for him at home. *I want Matty.*

His argument with her seemed trivial now. So she hadn't been right about the location of the gun. So what? Maybe they had it now. Brian didn't want her mad at him and wouldn't spend another night tossing and turning thinking about her. He would rather spend the night tossing and turning with her.

Chapter 10

I have to see her tonight. More than the usual brand of attraction to a woman propelled Brian out of the station house and into his car bound for Matty's house. A fire in his gut over a curvy body covered with satiny skin could be easily handled if the lady extended the invitation. But the embers Matty had stoked into flame encased in the Cat Woman costume burned inside Brian with a strange, prophetic intensity. Although he wanted that silken skin under his hands in spades, he wanted a deeper connection with her more—as if destined.

Certainly Matty's uncanny ability to peer into parallel worlds unsettled him, made him doubt his own instincts. A karmic aura surrounded her, mysterious, maybe off-putting to his practical nature. He should keep a professional arm's length, maybe a couple, from spooky Matty Connors. Instead he intended to wrap his arms around her, apologize for his outburst and offer the formerly infallible psychic whatever comfort he could over her first time failure.

Then, when back in her good graces, he would act on the compelling desire that had him racing into the twenty-four hour market for a consoling and please-forgive-me, dual purpose bouquet of roses. Choosing the most fragrant bunch, an unusual coffee color that reminded him of her eyes, he hustled out of the store to call at Matty's townhouse uninvited.

For the second time in the past few hours a front door opened to Brian before he rang the bell. "I knew you were coming," Matty greeted him, an uncharacteristic monotone in her soft voice.

A chill shuddered through him and he widened his eyes. "Of course you did."

Matty sighed. "I don't want to talk to you, Brian. Good night."

His left hand stopped the door she pushed forward in mid-arc. Watchdog Clyde at her feet growled with as much menace as a Boston terrier could muster. "Matty, I'm sorry." Thrusting the bouquet toward her with a contrite smile he continued, "Hear me out, OK? There's been another development in the case."

Arms folded across her chest, she glared at him like he strained her last shred of patience. She wore a Chicago Bears jersey that exposed all but a couple inches of upper thighs, long shapely legs, bare feet and pink toe nails. A muted drone of the game play-by-play filtered out to him on the stoop. The lady got points for choosing to watch football on a Monday night. Without any makeup on her face, her hair messy in a clip at the back of her head, her allure compared to her Halloween outfit should have diminished for Brian. Her affect on him the opposite, nothing about Matty was predictable.

"Brian, take your hand off the door, please."

Holding his arm stiff against the opposing force she exerted on the door, he'd beg if necessary. "Please, Matty, take the flowers and let me in."

She shook her head, put more muscle into wrestling the door closed. Clyde growled again, this time a pretty impressive effort.

Brian's bicep flexed, preventing the door from budging further. "We have the gun I believe Ben used to shoot Jake. Jodi Wilson is dead. The gun was found next to her body..."

"The gun isn't in the boxcar now." The monotone persisted.

Regretting that he probably caused her to be so dispirited, Brian asserted, his voice soft, "It's all right that you were wrong, Matty. Nobody's perfect."

Again he extended the bouquet towards her, a peace offering.

"Go away, Brian!" Her powerful shove on the door took him off guard and he jerked his arm forward to keep it open a couple inches.

"C'mon, Matty. Let me come in. Please."

"No." The pressure against the door didn't let up and Clyde set up a racket barking.

"If you close the door, I'll shout through it."

"The neighbors will call the police."

"Handy you have one on your doorstep."

"Oh, all right," she conceded with an exasperated emphasis on the last word. She released the door suddenly and Brian stumbled a few steps into her hallway.

Gracefully balancing on one sexy bare foot, Matty kicked the door shut behind him with the other. "Clyde, it's OK. Go back and take care of Bonnie." She stared down at the dog until he appeared satisfied that his mistress meant business and trotted toward the back of the house.

Glancing at Brian, Matty asserted, "The gun isn't in the boxcar now *and* said boxcar is *not* the one you found in the trailer. The gun *was* in the boxcar I described and that is my last word on—"

He smothered her monologue with his mouth. He hadn't aimed to squelch her words, nothing to do with words at all. Brian could not wait to taste her, explore that sensuous mouth and play out the fantasies that had spun him into her seductive web. Now linked to her lips, little mewling sounds she made in the back of her throat as she drew back, pulled him forward with her persisting in the kiss, pressing harder, delving further, until she answered exerting pressure of her own, smoldering, enticing, moaning a drawn out, "Mmmmmmmm."

Tilting her head back, she gazed at him, a dazed expression on her face, cocoa-colored eyes hooded, beckoning. Clasping her body close to his reflexively, his forearm against the small of her back, bouquet dangling in his right hand, Brian searched deep within Matty's eyes an elevator fall sensation at his core. "I had to see you. I'm sorry I didn't call first," he admitted, finding it difficult to breathe normally, still caught up in the kiss.

"I'm glad," she whispered, her heart pounding a rapid rhythm against his chest, her full lips parted in a lazy smile. "Did you only want to *see* me?"

"For starters." Brian tossed the flowers on the floor and grasped the hem of her jersey, hiking it up in one rapid motion. She aided him with the upward sweep of her arms and he skimmed the shirt off over her head exposing creamy perfect breasts, rosy nipples pebbled in arousal, scanty black lace bikinis an inviting V atop firm slender thighs. Her gaze level, naughty, she yanked his jacket off, blanketed the flowers with it. Next, tugging on his shirt at his waist, he saved her the trouble and whipped it over his head. Skin to skin, he relished her softness, each breath she took like a bellows fanning simmering flames into an inferno inside him. *More.* He lifted her up, her lace-covered bottom brushing his arm, her soft arms a sweet, gentle necklace.

Blood rushing like lava through his veins, Brian moved toward the staircase, bounded up the stairs, the exertion inciting biting need to wrap his body around hers, immerse, mate. She nibbled on his neck, rode pliant in his arms, her sweet scent intoxicating, her warm breath like feathers on his shoulder. Launching her to a soft landing on the first bed he found, he yanked his belt open, dispensed with it, his jeans, his briefs. Fully aroused, he still had enough willpower left to hold back and peer into her eyes in the dim light that shadowed her face, her dark eyes smoky, gleaming. "I want you, Matty."

With a sly smile she replied, "That's very obvious. I want you, too."

****

Her panties slid down her legs, his thumbs scraping the sides of her hips and legs, and she cupped her hands over the delicate exposed flesh to contain the fist of need that stole her breath. Gentle nudges on the inside of her knees parted her legs dangling over the side of the bed. Brian stepped between them, her inner thighs gripping his taut leg muscles. He arched over her like a tantalizing canopy just out of reach. His head bent over one breast and hovered, his tongue flicking puckers in her nipple that raced fiery sizzles straight to her center. Her arms at her sides in utter surrender breathing deeply, her breasts heaved up into the warm slickness of his tongue, down with feverish chills and back up, layer over layer of sensations. Greedy lust swelled inside her to taste his soap-scented skin.

With a throaty moan she encircled his torso pressing her hands on the hard, smooth plane of his broad back to draw his powerful body down, yearning to fuse him close. Ridges of muscle tightened beneath her palms resisting, withholding as he teased her breasts with his tongue in divine torture. She moaned again, arched her hips upward, grazing his erection.

He lowered his body over her, covering her completely, melding his lips to hers. Peppermint on her tongue, pulsing uncontrollable passion gripped her. Her fingers couldn't get enough of the textures of him, silky hair, course stubble on his cheeks, tender soft skin at the nape of his neck, ridged muscles down his back. His body heavy, she undulated beneath him, an urgent rhythm of varying pressures that swept her ever higher, pressed her ever closer to him until she had him inside her. On a gasp she accepted him, *exactly* what she wanted, needed. Locked together, her eyes clamped shut; she met each thrust, desire threatening to split her apart. He tensed and moved more frantically in unison with her, hearts pounding, breathing erratic. Ecstasy speared through her, bloomed ever upward and fired a piercing bolt of release as he joined her with a fierce burst of expelled breath.

Sated, delirious with pleasure, she floated down to reality like a feather on a hot summer breeze, the weight of Brian's lax body a welcome burden. Still joined with him, his radiant body heat enveloped her.

His breathing slowed and the heartbeat that had pounded along with hers, chest to chest, steadied. He didn't move, still linked together he whispered, "Lost and found."

Exactly. "Yes," Matty whispered.

Slowly he pushed up and rolled on his back, the inevitable disconnection still a little disappointment. Already Matty anticipated the next time they'd make love. She rolled on her side, propped her head on her hand, her elbow on a pillow.

He turned his head toward her, his eyes dark and earnest in her unlit bedroom. "Did I hurt you?"

Sighing, she replied, "If you did, feel free to hurt me again."

His perfect smile curled his lips, straight teeth so white compared to his shadowed cheeks where dimples budded. His lips straightened, his gaze intent. "I don't want to do this with you anymore."

Her heart lurched, stung with the blatant rejection. "Is this just about *sex* for you?"

A sudden sweep of his arms crushed her against his chest, squeezed. "I meant the case." He eased her back, her head on the pillow and rolled on his side to face her, his eyes soft, dimples creasing with his half-smile. "This..." He traced her bottom lip with his finger. "This I'd like to do all night long."

His lips brushed hers sweet, soft, possessive as the kiss deepened and stirred a dizzying swell of longing deep within her. Opening her eyes as their lips parted on a sigh she stared into his eyes, her vision hazy.

"Eyes are windows," he said, his gaze steady, gentle. "You lady, have the most beautiful soul I've ever seen."

"Ah, so poetic."

Brian returned her smile, those appealing dimples softening his face. "Oh, I can do better than that." His hand caressed the sweep of her throat, over a shoulder, across her breasts. "Your skin is a garden of Eden."

The tingling exploration continued, feather light, teasing. "Smells like a citrus orchard, silky and softer than anything else in this world—paradise."

Her eyes closed reflexively to blot out any reality but the tantalizing sensations his fingers incited. Now his lips retraced the trail his hand had followed from her throat, roaming over and down her body. Shuddering, exquisite longing stole her breath, stoked her mounting desire to have, to take. She pressed her hand over his, low on her belly where need gathered in pulsing knots.

"Look at me, Matty."

Her eyelids fluttered open, his eyes on hers dark, potent. "I'm going to make you mine."

Her heart leaped. *I already am.*

Rolling on top of her his lips met hers, crushing, bruising, feeding her need. Already the intimate dance with Brian had its own perfect rhythm, ageless, meant as if she had been his always. Nothing mattered but this ascent with him, the shattering climax fitting, awesome, utterly fulfilling.

On a groan he collapsed on her, his chest heaving against her breasts. She tightened her arms around him, stroked his broad back relishing the slide of her fingers over smooth, taut skin.

Blanketed by his body, Matty held him tight to

share this peaceful, quiet shelter. He raised his head and kissed her again, deeply, gently, no words necessary but this seal between them. Propping up on his elbows he searched her face, seemingly content just to look at her.

"Never before," he whispered.

She furrowed her brow, staring into his turquoise eyes to grasp his meaning. "Me, either," she replied.

Lying next to her, he grasped her hand, drew it towards his mouth, gently sucking each finger one by one.

She captured the tip of his finger between her teeth, a gentle playful bite. "Want to take a little...break? The Bears were actually winning."

Sitting up, she curled her legs beneath her in a lotus pose and tilted her head, expectant.

"Sure." He rolled and sat up, his long legs over the side of the bed, back to her. "We OK with you seeing me socially instead of professionally?"

She chuckled. "Are you asking me to be your girlfriend and leave the detective work to you?"

He twisted his head and, in profile, bit the corner of his lip. "Yes, I am."

Her heart fluttered. "Fine with me." Sliding off the other side of the bed, she scooped up her panties and put them on, grabbed a robe out of her closet and wrapped it around her. Tying the belt, she skirted the bed and stood in front of him. "It was never my case. Always yours."

Brian nodded, accepted the clothes she gathered up from the floor and handed to him. He held his briefs out in front of him by the waistband, jabbed each long leg into place and stretched them on as he stood. A zinger of desire shimmered through her and she almost tossed her robe off and attacked him.

"Did you see this truth?" He grinned gesturing to the rumpled bed.

Brian in a tuxedo. I thought he was dressed for

our wedding day. Maybe I thought right. "Perhaps I had a hint." She grinned at him, shimmying to imitate a victorious end zone dance. "Are you ready for a little football?"

His arm draped over her shoulder. "Go Bears."

Chapter 11

Ole man river. That ole man river. He just keeps.... I don't know the words to that one.

Um. OK.

"Rolling. He just keeps rolling along," Matilda sang as she jogged steadily on the leaves-strewn path.

Hey, you're there. Cool. What's that thudding sound? Are you pounding chicken or something?

"I'm running. Morning jog. Where are you, Jake?" Matilda pried her earphones out and let them dangle around her neck, her mind tuned to hear him. Good thing no other jogger was in sight or she might be pressed to explain talking to an invisible person.

That's the million-dollar question, now isn't it? Are you getting closer? The thumping seems louder. Where are you?

"On the Illinois Prairie Path parallel to Butterfield Road," she responded. "Just about to cross an arched bridge."

"Stop! Stop! Are you on the bridge?"

Matilda pulled up, breathless in the center of the bridge. Heartbeat hammering so hard her ears throbbed, she leaned over one side of the flat stone railing, then raced to the other side, scanning the flowing water, straining to see below the surface. "Talk to me, Jake. Please. I'm looking down at the river."

Bingo! Tell Mother she found me. And thanks for coming, lady.

Frozen, her legs stiff, her stomach a knot, Matilda focused on the banks, on the water's depths again, but detected nothing but clotted, mushy leaves along the muddy fringes of the river and a couple branches floating lazy under the bridge. "Jake? Jake! Where are you? I can't see you."

Nothing but the rustle of brittle leaves in the breeze, the crackle of dead leaves along the ground, under her running shoes. *Ah, shit.* Her heart sank in the silence, as she understood that Lexxie would face the ugly reality that now penetrated Matilda's consciousness. Brian and Joe had been searching for Jake's body, and they were right.

She leaned her elbows on the cold stone along the top edge of the bridge and stared into the brown, swirling water. Before this, today had started perfectly. Shaking her head sadly, last night seemed like a fantasy now. Did it really happen?

If she had given in to temptation when she awoke, indulged in the guilty pleasure of snuggling with Bonnie and Clyde under the warm comforter and ditched her usual ten-mile run, she wouldn't have faced this truth. She could have continued the delicious dreams of Brian's hands skimming over her, caressing, possessing. Last night Brian had awakened long dormant and then entirely new sensations in Matty.

Smiling, she recalled the lovely evening: scorching kisses, piercing longing, heavenly completion. The Bears had actually won. And not one single nightmare. Eric slept in peace and so, apparently, did Matty.

Heaving a sigh, Matilda slid her cell phone out of the holder clipped to her waistband and dialed Brian's cell. Her heart raced faster with each ring tone in her ear, a combined anticipation hearing his voice and trepidation convincing him that Jake had revealed this latest truth.

"Morning, Matty," came his deep voice, a sexy rumble that vibrated through her. "I was just going to call you. Are you free for dinner tonight?"

The knot in her stomach unraveled, a diving delightful sensation at the prospect but unfortunately she'd deal with another truth. "Brian, I've located Jake's body."

"What? Where?" His voiced drilled in her ear substituting the cool professional for the sensuous lover.

Matilda's heart lurched and dismay stabbed that her "personal relationship only agreement" with Brian had been so short lived.

This is for Jake.

"I'm on the stone bridge over the southwest tributary of the river." She paced down to the continuation of the path, reversed and back up over the arched bridge, then reversed back again. "I'll wait for you. How quickly can you be here?"

"What am I dealing with, Matty? Can you see his body?" Brian fired at her.

"No. I'm not certain of his exact location. Only that he brought me here and told me I found him."

"Oh... " His statement hung.

She waited for Brian to continue, still pacing as seconds passed. "Brian? Are you still there?"

"Yeah. So we're talking dredging the river?"

Matilda stopped and leaned over the six inch, flat railing again. Futile, but she hoped she'd detect something telling in the seemingly tranquil river. "I guess so. There's nothing on the banks as far as I can see."

"OK. Shit. OK. I'm on my way. Maybe ten minutes, fifteen tops. I'll make some calls."

Intuitively, she realized Brian accepted her truth begrudgingly and had apologized over the boxcar incident to appease her, not because he believed her. All that mattered was that he accepted the truth now—enough to act. "Thanks. See you in a few minutes."

****

Brian leaned against the kitchen counter

draining the last of his mug of coffee. He had not expected to start today or any day working the case with Matty and her "crystal ball" after last night. Sleep had evaded him when he had returned home from her house late last night and he lay in bed haunted by her lingering scent on his hands, reliving the sweet memory of lovemaking and hungering for more of her.

Another memory had bounced around in his brain all night. He had once asked his dad how he knew his mother was *the* one. John Sullivan's Irish eyes had twinkled, amused, and he and had replied on a chuckle, "Oh, you will know, my boy. The woman for you is the one who can bring you to your knees."

His father's pronouncement had remained a meaningless notion, almost nonsense to Brian until last night when he understood. *Matty is the one.* She could bring him to his knees, virtually had leveled him. Strange that it hadn't surprised him. Just the opposite. Eyes open, he had surrendered to her spell, reveled in the power she exerted over him.

Now this. Brian didn't want Matty involved in his work. He didn't want to doubt her or fight with her again. Caprisi would have him typing reports ten hours a day for the rest of his career if he squandered resources searching for Jake's body with as little to go on as conversations between Matty Connors and the great beyond.

Still he couldn't overlook the information, had to investigate. *How do I play this?* He scrolled through his contacts and punched the call button on his cell phone.

"Hey, Ed. It's Brian Sullivan."

"Hey, Brian. What's up? Ready to admit defeat?"

"Never. It was a tie game and stays that way."

Brian and Ed were on opposite all-star teams in a charity softball game that ended in a tie when half of Brian's team had to respond to a five-car pile up on Roosevelt Road.

"Lucky for you half your team was called away before we could stomp you into the ground."

"There's always next season. Ed, I have a favor to ask."

"Name it."

"I want to keep this under the radar. I have my reasons." Brian hesitated, considering how much to divulge. "I have a lead from a psychic named Matty Connors..."

"Holy shit. *Matty Connors*? What the hell is she doing in Illinois?"

"You've heard of her?"

"Are you kidding? I took a course on psychics and their assistance in cases at the Academy. Every other case we discussed involved her. I'd love to meet her."

I must have had my head up my ass when I was at the Academy. "Well, today is your lucky day. Matty is waiting for me on the stone bridge over the river, near Butterfield Road. She *heard* a missing kid in the water. His name is Jake Ashford. We've been looking for him for months."

"Heard about the case. Mountains of political bullshit. You don't sound convinced this is a credible lead."

"You know me. I'm a black and white kind of guy."

"Me, too. But if Matty Connors tells me there's a body in the river, then there's a body in the river. I'll give Pete a call, too. We'll be there in about ten minutes."

"Thanks, Ed. I appreciate it."

Brian dialed Joe's number next and filled him in.

****

Matilda stomped her feet and dug her hands deeper into her sweatshirt pockets. The trees dressed in fading fall colors would soon be gray and bare. Winter wasn't far away and if she didn't start jogging she'd be frozen like a statue on the bridge when the first snow arrived.

She tugged her phone off the belt clip, about to call Brian again when a white van's tires crunched along the gravel path in front of her, followed by Brian's jeep. Her heart swelled, eager to see Brian unfurl that gorgeous body out of his car. A warm blush traveled up her neck as she enjoyed observing him emerge into the dappled sunlight. After executing several eye-catching powerful strides, he greeted two tall men clad in black divers' suits as they jumped out of the van. The three men sauntered towards her, but her eyes remained riveted on Brian. Relieved that he directed a sunny smile at her, his sea-blue eyes shining, Matilda's anxiety evaporated.

"Matty this is Ed Kelly and Pete Sarnelli, two of Chicago PD's best divers."

"Good to meet you." Matilda held out a hand toward Ed Kelly.

"I am honored to meet you Miss Connors." Her eyes widened and she glanced at Brian, alarmed, as Kelly's beefy hand grasped hers and pumped it, the flesh of his wrist bulging over the black cuff of his diver's suit. "Your hand's cold," he remarked with a smile as warm as the hand that encased hers.

"Been out here a while." Matilda shook Pete Sarnelli's huge warm hand next, her fingers thawing some as she continued to stare at Brian who apparently was unfazed that he had revealed her identity to two more of "Chicago's finest."

"It's a privilege to shake your hand, Miss Connors," Sarnelli stated.

"Please call me Matty. Nice to meet you," she managed to remain polite, itching to talk to Brian privately, outrage building underneath her forced courtesy.

"Brian filled us in a little. What do you want us

to do?" Pete brushed past her, stopped mid-bridge and peered over the edge at the water. "Do you have an idea where you want us to start the dive?"

Matilda temporarily dispensed with confronting Brian about his breach of confidentiality, used to directing the police at crime scenes. This had been her life in California. No one had doubted her after they had worked with her once. They took her truths as fact and acted on her counsel. "My strong impression is start under the bridge and move out towards the waterfall."

"Let's go." Pete and Ed went back to the van to get their equipment leaving Brian and Matty alone on the bridge.

"Hi." Brian leaned down and touched his lips to hers, a slow melting kiss. She closed her eyes warmed through and through, nothing more important that moment than the connection to the man who owned her heart.

****

One eye on the van, Brian ended the kiss gently before Kelly and Sarnelli witnessed the lip-lock.

"I was afraid you wouldn't come." Her words slapped Brian.

"You have to know I would always come if you call. I'm really sorry I've given you reason to think otherwise."

"I understand. This takes some getting used to." Her calm, brown eyes enthralled him. This thing of hers, this gift that she shared couldn't be easy to live with. Especially faced with lug-heads like him who couldn't fathom how her "truths" could possibly be true.

Ed and Pete trod forward, diving masks and flippers dangling in their hands, bulbous air tanks on their backs. Matty rubbed her arms with her hands. "Why'd you tell them my name, Brian?"

"It just slipped out. I had no idea your reputation was common knowledge on the force,"

Brian admitted. "Don't worry about them. They will keep your involvement to themselves. I trust them with my life."

She nodded assent. "All right."

Brian watched the divers slide down the riverbank and submerge, Matty shivering at his side. Slipping his jacket off, he draped it over her shoulders, secured it in place by wrapping one arm around her. Minutes passed as bubbles rose to the surface and moved systematically under the bridge disappearing from his vantage point on one side of the bridge. He steered Matty over to the far side, picking up the trail of bubbles in a widening grid toward the horseshoe waterfall.

Pete broke the surface of the water and yanked the mouthpiece out, bobbing like an overgrown seal. "Sullivan, call Caprisi! We got something."

"Found you, Jake," Matty whispered and tilted her face up toward him, eyes brimming.

Water lapped against the riverbanks and the falls rushed behind the diver, the sounds cascading in Brian's ears as disbelief and elation warred within him. "I'll be damned."

With one arm Brian lifted Matty off her feet. He shifted his hold, folding her inward and pressed her to his chest, breathed in a lungful of her soft scent. She giggled, a tremulous quaking against him that heightened his elation and kept disbelief at bay. Setting her down, he grinned at her, his face inches away from hers. If Pete weren't a few yards away, he'd kiss her senseless.

"I'm on that Sarnelli," Brian called out as he dug in his pocket for a phone.

Calls made. Brian climbed up the banks to the path, hiked up toward Matty on the bridge and wrapped her in his arms. "You don't have to stay."

"Good." Her voice muffled against his chest. Angling her head up, she assessed him. "The less people who know I was here the better." She cast a dubious glance at Ed and Pete who sat comfortably on the bank below waiting for their team to help with the reclamation of the sleeping bag they had found chained to a cinder block at the bottom of the river.

"They won't talk to the press. Have no fear. They hate the bastards." Brian laughed. "Let me drive you home."

"No thanks. I want to finish my run and get to the office. Shamus will send out a hunting party for me if I don't get in gear." She stood on tiptoe and pressed cold lips against his. Instant warmth sparked.

He'd like to linger in the kiss, vamp up the heat, but he'd save that for later. Brian cupped her heart-shaped face in his hands and promised himself he'd steep in the tender softness of her skin as soon as he could. "Thank you for last night."

She beamed at him, impish. "I had a nice time."

Brian looked at her askance. "Nice? Is that the best adjective you can come up with?"

Her eyes darted at distant sounds beyond the tree line—tires braking, gravel churning, and car doors slamming.

"You go ahead." Brian released his arms, accepted his jacket back from her. "I'll call as soon as I know anything."

Matty jogged off in the opposite direction and Brian watched her retreat, appreciating her graceful form. He turned away grudgingly when Joe walked up behind him.

"Did she find Jake?" Brian turned around again and viewed Matty's figure shrinking in the distance.

"I don't know. Ed and Pete found a sleeping bag on the bottom."

"Let's go talk to the ME."

Brian and Joe hiked down the slippery bank

toward the medical examiner standing at river edge, boots smeared with mud. Yellow police tape flapped around the branches and looped around the trunks of perimeter trees. The diving team worked a winch that brought up a sodden sleeping bag. Disengaging the lines, four guys maneuvered the bag toward shore, hauled it out of the water and placed it on top of a body bag stretched out on the sloping ground.

The ME squatted, tried to work the zipper. "A little help here." A latex-gloved subordinate knelt down on the other side of the bag and plied industrial shears along the zipper track, unfolding the material carefully, exposing human remains.

"Decomposition is extensive. Been here a while. Don't jostle anything further. Let's zip the body bag around the sleeping bag." He stood, tugged off his gloves. "I'll know more when I get it back to the morgue. I know, I know, Sullivan," he addressed Brian without looking at him. "You need the results yesterday. I'll do what I can. Any connection to the dead girl I have back in the cooler?"

"I don't know. You tell me."

"I'll start on this as soon as I get back. Caprisi put a red flag on it. Even allowing overtime. Must be important for him to open the old wallet."

The body was loaded into the ME's van and he drove away.

Brian and Joe remained behind with Kelly and Sarnelli to lend a hand carrying equipment back up to their van.

Pete slammed the cargo doors shut.

"Thanks for your help guys. I owe you," Brian said.

"We'll hold you to that," Ed promised.

"It was a pleasure meeting Matty Connors. Wouldn't mind working again with her," Sarnelli remarked.

"You never met Matty Connors and she's not connected to this operation. Got it?" Brian brought the point home.

"Yeah, we get it. Call me if you need me." Pete faked-punched Brian's shoulder and opened the passenger door of the van. Gravel crunched as Ed cut ruts in the ground driving the van in reverse off-path around Brian's jeep.

"All we can do now is wait." Joe stared at the river, thumbs hooked in his pockets. "How did Matty know Jake was there?"

"We don't know it's Jake."

Joe faced him. "It's Jake."

"She heard him, she said. Led her right to the spot." Brian shook his head.

"Amazing, isn't it?"

Brian nodded. "Unbelievable."

"You still having problems accepting her abilities?"

Brian shrugged his shoulders. "I apologized last night for accusing her of being wrong about the gun in the train. She still insists she wasn't."

"I wouldn't doubt it. We'll find a connection. You wait and see. Things are falling into place. I got a call from Forensics on my way over. The fingerprints on the gun found at the Wilson murder match Ben Jarvis. The DA is on it. Caprisi put pressure on our droll ME to rush the autopsy. Get the bullet over to forensics. Now that we have Jake we'll be able to tie it all together."

"If it's Jake."

"It's Jake." Joe clapped a hand on Brian's shoulder. "You hungry? I'm starving. Want to grab something to eat?"

"I could go for some pancakes. Only had time for coffee so far today."

"Let's go." Joe hung his arm over Brian's shoulder. "You can tell me all about your apology last night to Matty Connors."

Chapter 12

Caprisi looked downright jovial. Brian could swear he detected creases in the man's cheeks on either side of his full lips. Eyebrows arched, Brian sat where indicated in front of the commander's desk.

"Well, Sullivan." Caprisi folded his hands, leaned his elbows on his desk in a let's-have-a-friendly-chat posture. "I no longer regret my decision to designate you lead investigator on the Ashford case."

A backhanded compliment but he'd take it. "Thank you, sir."

The creases on Caprisi's face deepened, just a hint of movement toward a real smile. "You going to tell me how you found the body?" The commander's lips repositioned in a straight line, a penetrating gleam in his hazel eyes.

"Sure." Brian trained his eyes on Caprisi's. "A lead from a jogger on the Prairie Path."

Unflinching, Caprisi sat back in his chair, hands still folded on the desk. "A jogger." He took a sip from a mug that read, World's Best Daddy. "Want some coffee, Sullivan?"

"I'm good, sir."

Setting the mug down, Caprisi leaned forward again, stared. "So a jogger was...jogging along on a bridge ten feet above the river and noticed a sleeping bag anchored on said river bottom and knew the thing to do was call Brian Sullivan, lead investigator on the Ashford case."

Brian grinned. "Guess so, sir."

The commander's eyes darkened, his jaw

clenched. "And where is this jogger now? I'd like to meet him...or her. Shake his/her hand."

Dead serious, Brian replied, "He/she just jogged away I suppose after making an anonymous call to me."

Caprisi shoved up from his chair, paced a couple times behind his desk, looked out the window as he continued, "I notified Mrs. Ashford-Whitman personally last evening that the body has been identified as her son."

"Yes, sir, I know."

"You've seen the reports, I take it?"

"Haven't slept for two days pushing the ME, forensics, ballistics." Brian ran a hand over his chin, scratchy with beard stubble. "I could use a shave."

"Are you working with the DA?"

"We're tied at the hip. Ben Jarvis is being moved to the city lock-up this morning. The DA is going for indictments on two counts, first degree." Brian stifled a yawn and straightened from a sliding slouch in the chair. "Anything else, sir?"

Caprisi faced Brian again, eyes gleaming. "I don't know how the hell you pulled this off. But good work, Sullivan. That will be all."

"Thank you, sir." Brian rose and strolled out of Caprisi's office toward his desk. A uniformed Chicago PD officer intercepted him.

"You Sullivan?"

"One of them," Brian answered. "Brian. What can I do for you?"

"I'm here to transport the Jarvis kid. He won't budge until he talks to you."

"Really?" Brian folded his arms. "Is his lawyer here, too?"

"Nope. What do you want me to do?"

"Let's go see what he has to say."

Brian walked briskly at the officer's side, down a flight of stairs, through the security gate into the holding cell area. Ben Jarvis hunched over on his haunches in the corner of a cell, a squatting fetal position. He raised his head as the two men approached, his eyes bloodshot, the face of abject misery. Brian paused, watched him rise and limp over to the bars.

"You've gotta help me, man," Ben implored, tears welling, hands wrapped around the bars. "I didn't do this. I don't know how Jake wound up in a river. *I didn't put him there! I didn't kill Jodi! I loved her!*"

Gorge rose in Brian's throat as he hastened to stand in front of Ben, face planted inches from Ben's. "You piece of shit. You shot them both and we have proof. I have nothing to say to you."

Brian turned his back on the criminal, strode away.

"Wait! Wait!"

Brian glanced over his shoulder and saw Ben double over, hysterical now. "I admit I did shoot Jake," he blubbered. "I ran away. It was an accident." Snot poured out of the kid's nose into the corners of his lips. "He was gone when I got back to the trailer."

Brian walked back toward the cell, firing accusations with each step, "We know you shot Jake, *twice*. His blood is on your rug. The bullets were fired from the gun we found next to Jodi Wilson's dead body. Your prints are on the gun. We found you fleeing the scene. I guess you ran away from that *accident*, too."

"Please, please," Ben whimpered. "I didn't do this. Help me..."

Brian turned to the uniform cop. "He's all yours." He strode away, took the stairs up three at a time to work off some of the adrenaline that pumped through his aching head. *Lying sack of shit.*

Back on the first floor he navigated around desks in the squad room and plopped down behind his, head in hands.

****

Matilda grabbed two potholders and slid the casserole out of the oven, setting it on the granite countertop. Enticing breakfast smells permeated her kitchen: eggs, melted cheddar cheese, pork sausage. The casserole recipe was one of her favorites. She planned to wrap the pan in foil and when it cooled enough to touch, bring breakfast for two to the Windsor Village Police Station. Hurried phone calls from Brian to break two dinner dates preceded her brainstorm to share this morning meal with him.

He had thanked her last evening for indeed finding Jake and ended the conversation with, "I miss you."

And she sorely missed him, although she fully understood the necessity for him to work insane hours bringing Jake's killer to justice.

It's just that I'm not sure they've found him yet.

The truth that Jake had given her before he led her to his grave in the river spooled in her mind. Jake had talked to somebody after Ben shot him in the leg. Was it Ben? It could have been based on the exchange. She wasn't sure.

The location of the gun in the train set had to be the key. But the puzzle pieces still didn't fit for Matilda. Try as she might she couldn't get Jake to talk to her further. *Jake, please tell me who killed you. Who put your body in the river? Why don't you just tell me?*

Of course, her pleas to Jake in the next world went nowhere. Matilda couldn't will truths to her any more than she could will them away. Satisfied that Jake's body had been found and conclusive evidence was mounting, she resolved not to think about the case further. Then, maybe Jake would come to her one more time.

Testing the side of the pan with her fingertip without burning it, she tore off a sheet of foil and wrapped the pan. "Hey guys," she called to her dogs, although only Clyde's ears pricked up at her voice. "Let's go."

Her entourage settled in the back seat and the casserole stowed on the passenger seat, Matilda drove to the clinic and dropped the dogs off before continuing to the police station. At a little before nine AM, traffic clogged the main roads. She chose back routes, meandering through subdivisions where speed limits were sometimes only twenty mph.

Humming along with Leona Lewis, *Bleeding Love*, she swayed to the music, eyes on the road, alert for school kids. The casserole on the seat still smelled appetizing, and she was fairly sure there'd be a microwave at the station house to warm it up. Happy that she'd spend time with Brian, her heart quickened. She didn't need visions of him in a tuxedo on what might be their wedding day to know she was in love with him. That truth coursed through her blood with every heartbeat.

Her heartbeat raced as she neared his desk. Clothes rumpled, sandy brown whiskers shadowing his face, Brian's greenish-blue eyes brimmed with delight when he caught sight of her, a wondrous welcome.

"Hey, beautiful," he greeted her, his voice soft as a caress.

Aware that this was his workplace, she resisted dumping the casserole on his desk so she could fly into his arms. Instead, she lowered the pan carefully to the desktop and primly sat down on the chair at the side of his desk. "I brought us breakfast." She glanced at the pan. "It might still be warm."

Brian removed the foil from the pan with one swipe of his arm, a movement that transfixed her attention to his large hand. A sensual rush blasted through her remembering what that roving hand could do to her body.

****

A minute later, Nagle ushered the Whitmans

over to him—unannounced visitors that at that moment made Brian grind his teeth.

He forced a smile at the couple and rose to greet them. "My deepest condolences on your loss."

Alexis Ashford-Whitman's sad eyes pinched Brian's heart. "Thank you."

"Lexxie!" Matty jumped up, rounded the chair and flung her arms around Mrs. Ashford-Whitman. "I'm so so sorry. Please, if there's anything I can do…"

James Whitman stood, soldier at ease, his face grim while observing his sobbing wife in Matty's arms. He flicked his eyes in Brian's direction. "We're here for Jake. The funeral director is parked outside. Can you direct him to where…?" Whitman cast his eyes downward and then riveted them on Brian, his lips pursed in a grim line.

Brian frowned as Mrs. Ashford-Whitman and Matty joined Whitman in staring at him. "Uh. Let me direct you all to a conference room. Ms. Connors just brought breakfast to me. Perhaps we could share a meal?"

"I don't think I could eat." Mrs. Whitman clasped her hands together, rotated them against each other, shaking nervous circles.

Brian patted her shoulder. "It's OK, ma'am. Let's just go over here where we can talk privately."

Matty picked up the pan and walked beside him into the conference room, the Whitmans trailing behind. *She shouldn't be in this meeting but I can't leave her alone at my desk. Caprisi will home in on her in ten seconds.*

Brian closed the door and waited for the Whitmans to choose seats and then positioned at the table across from them. Matty deposited the pan on the far end of the table with a helpless shrug of her shoulders and then sat in a chair in a corner, away from the table.

"I apologize but I didn't expect you this morning

and I don't have Jake's personal effects ready for release."

"Personal effects?" Jake's mother trembled and tears streamed down her face, close to collapse, Brian judged.

"Yes, ma'am," Brian said carefully. "A watch, a ring and a holy medal, I believe."

"Oh." She bent her head and her shoulders shook as she wept.

"I'm afraid we can't release his body for burial, either. And I don't have a projected release date yet for you." *There was no easy way to say this.* "His body will be required to remain in the morgue until evidence is gathered to try the suspect, Ben Jarvis, for Jake's murder."

"Oh..." Mrs. Whitman appeared to swoon, sagging sideways toward Whitman.

Her husband slid an arm around her and let her lean heavily against his side, kissing the crown of her head. "It's all right, darling. Ssh. It's all right."

Brian stretched a hand over the table, a useless consoling gesture that the couple ignored.

"He didn't do it!" Matty exclaimed as she jumped up and scurried over to stand next to Mrs. Whitman's seat.

"Matty, sit down." Brian stared at her aghast. *What the hell is she saying?*

Jake's parents turned their attention to Matty wearing expressions on their faces as utterly flabbergasted as Brian supposed he wore.

"Ben didn't kill Jake. I just know it. I was confused before..." Matty ignored Brian's attempt to silence her with a look, although he knew she could see his face out of the corner of her eye.

"What the hell is this?" Whitman's commanding voice boomed and Brian cringed. *Caprisi will be all over this if he doesn't lower his voice.*

I have to take control of this meeting. "Calm down..."

"I saw Jake injured, talking to someone, thanking him for coming..." Matty blurted, flushed, adamant.

"What do you mean you *saw Jake?*" Whitman demanded.

"Matty..." Brian attempted again to restore rationality.

"She's the psychic who gave me the letter from Jake," Mrs. Whitman interjected. "Remember? Matilda Connors? She's Shamus Connors' partner. The vet where I take Jake's dog, Max."

Matty stared at her forcefully, her body tense and with an urgent tone in her voice continued, "I thought Ben came back. It had to be him. But now..."

"Matty sit down and be quiet!" Brian drilled out the order and guilt instantly punched him in the gut as his shout echoed.

She froze, turned her face toward him, her steely gaze tempered only by the tears that brimmed in her eyes. Yanking a chair away from the table she sank to the seat unblinking, her mouth clamped shut.

Mrs. Ashford-Whitman grabbed Matty's hand. "I thought you stopped working with Detective Sullivan to find my son."

Matty shook her head still staring at Brian, her injured expression a knife in his heart. "I found the location of Jake's body, Lexxie," she whispered.

Lexxie closed her eyes at the news, opened them slowly, her pale face grief-stricken. "And Jake has come to you again and exonerated Ben?"

Shaking her head again, Matty replied, "Not recently. But I know in my heart that whomever Jake spoke to in my vision wasn't Ben."

"I'm so glad. I just couldn't accept that the little boy who had sleepovers with my Jake could have grown into a man who could kill his best friend in cold blood."

The glimmer of happiness on the mother's face was a stark contrast to Brian's reaction to this reversal.

"You're sure?" Mrs. Whitman asked, her voice tremulous. "Jake made this clear?"

"No." Matty shook her head, her huge eyes sad. "It's a strong impression..."

"I've heard enough," Whitman asserted, his scowl menacing. Jabbing an index finger on the table repeatedly he addressed Brian. "Your commander told us that the body of evidence against Ben Jarvis was conclusive. That he would be punished for his crimes. What the hell kind of a police department is he running? *Psychics?* You've got to be fucking kidding."

"James!" his wife admonished him.

He glanced at his wife, his eyes soft. "Sorry for the language, Lexxie. But *seriously?*" He turned toward Brian a disdainful expression on his face.

"Ms. Connors, I'm going to have to ask you to leave," Brian requested in a monotone. He had no choice.

"But Brian...Detective Sullivan. I'm right about this." Her chest heaved and she winced defensively, Brian's indictment for his crime of squarely punching her in the jaw.

The boxcar incident hung between them and Brian was fully aware he stood on a swinging tightrope. The evidence and her truths didn't line up. He had spent two sleepless nights with the best of the best forensics experts in the city. Only one set of fingerprints was on the gun that killed both Jake and Jodi. Ben had tried to scrub Jake's bloodstains off the rug in his trailer and hadn't succeeded. Matty herself had "seen" Ben confront Jake, gun in hand, heard the killing shot. They had the gun, no thanks to Matty. She had been wrong about its location. She was wrong about this.

Brian dove off the tightrope without a net.

"Again, Ms. Connors, please leave. Your involvement with this case is over."

Those hypnotizing, innocent brown eyes never left Brian's face as she gently dropped Mrs. Whitman's hand and rose from her seat, her back ramrod straight. Her graceful movements, the sheen of tears in her eyes broke his heart. He prayed their love—yes love, he knew it with certainty—could survive his rejection of her confused truths. He'd never voluntarily test something so new for him, so fragile, but she left him no choice.

Matty advanced toward the conference room door and then glanced back over her shoulder. "I'm glad I could help find Jake and again I'm so sorry for your loss, Lexxie, Mr. Whitman." With the signature eerie glimmer in her eyes she gazed at Brian, an intense, private message directed at him that he read as, good-bye.

The door clicked behind her. Tempted to abandon the Whitmans and rush after her, Brian's professional discipline prevailed. "I assure you, the evidence points to our having your son's killer in custody. I ask respectfully for your patience. I'll do everything I can to expedite Jake's return to you so you may lay him to rest."

Brian rose and escorted the Whitman's out of the station house, unspeaking while his internal voice was anything but silent. "I didn't do this. Help me," Jarvis had pleaded. Brian had no reason to believe the kid; he had lied before, and would continue to lie right up until he was sentenced for the crimes he sure as hell had committed. All along Brian had distrusted Ben Jarvis. Had that made him predisposed to buy into Matty's original truth about the shooting? Now she was taking that back?

The contradictions plagued him and again he grappled with the dark gray area where Matty's visions imprisoned him, instead of the tidy cause and effect, black-and-white life he had inhabited before she had turned everything inside out.

Her visions weren't the only things that had turned Brian inside out. *I love her, that's the truth. But how do I love her if I don't believe her? Faced with my distrust, how could she love me?*

Exhausted and dispirited he resented that she had him in this conflicted state with the case front and center. He should be out celebrating. Case closed. The judicial system would take over from here. With nothing more to go on than *the* Matty Connors' strong impression, Brian picked up his phone and called the city lockup.

After navigating the bureaucratic hierarchy he left a message for Ben Jarvis. "Ask him if he still wants to talk to me alone. I'm going home for a shower and shave. Call my cell phone number, 630-555-3493. I can get down there with around thirty minutes lead-time. Thanks."

Chapter 13

Brian stomped into Joe's empty office to escape the head-splitting din of ever-ringing department phones, slamming the door behind him. The hollow door whacked home, upping the noise level in the squad room and ratcheting up Brian's agitation another notch. He wanted to punch something, anything to vent his frustration with Matty on inanimate things. She had made a fool of him with the Whitmans. Hadn't he made it clear how sensitive the case was, how "kid-gloves" treatment the marching orders had been for six endless months?

The brief ice cold shower had done nothing to relieve the stress building in Brian's chest like a constricting iron band. He wanted Matty in his life with a foreign, deepening need that made him question his sanity. She'd *have* to stay out of his professional life or she'd drive him nuts for real. Her suppositions, her "strong impressions" *had* to be curtailed. Yes, her truth had led them to Jimmy's murderer. Yes, she had found Jake's body and a long list of missing souls over the years. *But can't she write anonymous letters to the Chief of Police and leave me the hell out of it?*

The dark sky heavy with storm clouds visible through the office window fit his mood. The rain streaked glass reflected shower wet hair curled around his ears and a scowl on his face. Was it even possible to have Matty in his life? Would she want to be in his life anymore? After calling her cell phone several times all day and minutes earlier on the way back to the squad room he doubted it. The calls had routed directly to voice mail; the lady was obviously pissed. Would she ever speak to him again?

Leaning his head against the cool glass, he harnessed doubts about Matty and acknowledged nagging doubts about the case that *she* had planted like a slap in his face. The evidence pointed at Ben Jarvis and Brian had been satisfied—no elated— that it was conclusive. Ben's sniveling hadn't permeated Brian's belief that he was guilty—in fact, his lies cemented it. But then Matty's pronouncement and his certainty had eroded against his will.

His cell phone chirped. The meeting with Ben was set. Brian flipped the light switch off and rushed out to the parking lot, fat rain drops bouncing off his leather jacket.

Joe leaned against the passenger door of his jeep, oblivious to the elements. "Hey little brother." He swung the door open. "Thought you could use some company."

"Thanks." Brian rounded the rear of the car and slid in beside Joe.

"You all right?"

"Yeah. I'm OK." Brian fit the car key in the ignition switch, turned it and the engine growled. One arm draped over the wheel, he stared out the windshield, engine idling.

"You didn't sound OK when you called. We're heading downtown to question Jarvis, right?"

Brian nodded.

"Then you believe Matty."

Brian twisted his head toward Joe and rolled his eyes. "Are you kidding me? Her completely unfounded creepy intuition made me look like an idiot." Brian pulled away from the curb into the light traffic in front of the station house. "How can you be so calm?"

"Stop one minute and think this through. Why did she blurt out that Ben didn't kill Jake?"

Brian slapped a hand on the steering wheel, the stinging somehow welcome. "I sure as hell wish I knew."

"For God's sake, Brian. Focus on this woman's abilities. She said Ben didn't kill Jake because Ben didn't kill Jake. We have to face the fact that we still have a killer on the loose."

"Tell me one thing. How can you do it?" The traffic light on the Eisenhower Expressway entrance ramp turned green and Brian accelerated to merge with the fast moving stream of cars. "How can you just take every word of this stuff as fact? You don't have a problem throwing all the evidence in the garbage?"

"Nope. I want to capture the killer. She says we don't have him yet and that's good enough for me."

Brian huffed, head aching. "After all this, you're still convinced she's seeing Jake's karma, fate, whatever?" Riding the shoulder he pressed hard on the pedal increasing the speed to 65, 70, 75, the forward momentum pressing him back hard in his seat, satisfying. "Am I the only one who remembers coming up empty, searching the trailer for the gun on her say so?"

"That still remains to be seen," Joe remarked a little too smugly for Brian.

"Ach..."Brian concentrated on driving, silent and brooding, the circular conversation sour on his tongue.

"I know what it's like to be kicked in the gut by the woman you love." Joe's tone was matter of fact, classic Sullivan brother to brother. "Don't deny it. You're in love with Matty."

"Love sucks," Brian admitted, turning left off Congress.

"Tell me about it. But it's the best thing in the world, too. I wouldn't change my life." Brian parked at the curb, the jail a cinder block obelisk with slits for windows looming through the passenger window.

134

"But you don't have to worry about Bobbie interfering with your job. Let's go."

Brian checked the side mirror waiting for traffic to clear before he opened the door and met Joe on the sidewalk.

"I called Patrick after I heard from you this morning and he might be able to pave the way for us here. Pull a few strings."

"Good thinking. I haven't talked to him lately. Have they set the trial date for his case yet?"

"Next month I think. Speak of the devil." Joe smiled as their brother pushed through the revolving front door and loped down the steps. Joe grabbed Patrick's hand for a shake and Brian greeted his younger brother with a handshake and a pat on the back. A burst of pride and solidarity filled Brian standing as one with his brothers.

"How's my little niece doing? Keeping you up nights?" Pat gave Joe a wry smile.

"No, she is amazing, already sleeping through the night." Joe's face brightened with a grin.

Patrick turned and mounted the stairs, Brian and Joe on either side of him. "I took the twins to the movies last weekend. Who is Hannah Montana anyway?"

"I don't have a clue," Joe said. "Wait until I tell Bobbie that Uncle Patrick is available for babysitting."

"No way. I only baby sit for nieces and nephews over five years old. Kay had something at school for Mikey and asked me to take the girls. Don't tell them but I really enjoyed being with them. How's your psychic, Brian?"

"Touchy subject. No comment." Brian stomped his feet and blew on his hands all business letting Patrick, then Joe push through the revolving door in front of him.

Inside, Patrick informed him, "I've got the suspect in an interrogation room for you. He's a cocky bastard."

"I'll scare that cockiness right out of him, trust me," Brian growled, shrugging out of his jacket and folding it over his arm.

Patrick's deep blue eyes questioned Joe who just shook his head.

"Let's go and get this over with." Brian bounded up the stairs with his brothers trailing behind.

Patrick led Brian and Joe to a door with a cloudy window. Brian peered through it. Ben sat in a wooden arm chair slumped over a narrow table.

"I have to get back to work." Patrick patted Brian on the back. "Call me if you need anything."

"Thanks, Pat."

"You have to come for dinner and see Emma soon."

"Sure, Joe. Call me."

Brian yanked the door open and strode into the stifling hot room, Joe close behind. An ancient radiator panel in the corner noisily blasted hot dusty air. Brian tossed his jacket on one end of the table and Joe followed suit.

"You wanted to talk to me? Talk," Brian commanded Ben.

"I changed my mind. I have nothing to say without my lawyer." His hooded eyes transmitted hostility.

"You little shit." Brian rushed forward and grabbed Ben by his sweat-soaked, orange shirt, heaved him off the chair, toppling it, and slammed him into the wall. "Don't fuck with me."

"Brian, don't. Sit him down." Joe righted the chair.

Complying Brian tossed Ben back in the chair and then paced, a caged tiger ready to pounce.

Ben's eyes tracked Brian's every move, jaw clenched. "I get it. Good cop, bad cop. You guys are so predictable."

Joe put his hands on the arms of Ben's chair,

leaned his nose a scant inch from the kid's and stared into his watery, bloodshot eyes. "You got it wrong, pal. We're going to call your lawyer. Nice and official for the record. While we're waiting for him to get here, I'll be Brian's witness. Just in case you make the first move on him. No matter what he does to you, he's gotta protect himself. Got it?"

Sweat beaded on Ben's upper lip. "I get it."

Joe pushed off the chair, grimacing with distaste. Then he leaned against the wall and crossed his arms in front of his chest. "Have somebody call the lawyer," Joe said, off-handedly.

Brian made a move toward the door.

"No wait," Ben mumbled.

Brian halted. "You're trying my patience now. Lawyer or no lawyer, you're going away and I'll make sure they throw away the key."

"No lawyer. Please listen." Ben bent his head, wagged it, a seemingly humble supplicant now.

Brian pulled an armless chair out from the table and straddled it facing Ben. Joe strolled over to the table, pushed the play and record buttons on the tape machine and edged it close to Ben.

"Detective Brian Sullivan and Senior Detective Joseph Sullivan WVPD Homicide questioning suspect Benjamin Jarvis, November 5, 2009. Case number 297465003-26," Brian stated. "Benjamin Jarvis have you been read your rights?"

"Yeah."

"And you have waived your right to have an attorney present during questioning today?"

Ben nodded.

"Respond in the negative or affirmative for the recording, please," Brian demanded.

"Yeah. Yes."

"You requested this meeting. Proceed." Brian folded his arms over the chair back, rested his chin on his wrists and stared at Ben.

"This is the truth, man." Ben sweated openly

now, thin rivulets streaking his cheeks, his shirt across the chest and at the underarms, dark blotches of perspiration. "I shot Jake but I *didn't* kill him. It was an accident. We were high. I owed him money for the drugs. He owed money to the dealer and he couldn't pay up. He was a heavy user and snorted half his inventory himself. He lived with us for free, ate our food, still he kept hounding me for money. He came on strong and we argued. I was waving the gun around showing off and it fired. I didn't mean to shoot him, I just wanted to scare him. I shot him in the leg. Ask Jodi she..." Ben stiffened, his face crumbled. He bent over, head in hands. "I didn't kill Jodi. I loved her. She's all I have. What am I going to do without her?" He sobbed.

"Where'd you get the gun?" Brian asked, unmoved by the display.

Ben raised his head, wiped snot on his bare arm. "I stole it from my old man. He's retired police, Carbondale. I was going to hock it to pay Jake."

"Nice," Brian uttered under his breath. "Tell me what happened after that first shot."

"I only shot the gun once. I was in shock that I pulled the trigger. Jake yelled, cursed said, 'Are you fucking kidding me?' And then he laughed. We both laughed."

"You shot him in the leg and he laughed?"

"We were high. We thought it was funny."

Fucking stupid kids. "What happened next?"

"Jodi didn't think it was funny and she pulled me out the door."

"Was she high, too?"

Ben hung his head. "Nah. She was the best thing that ever happened to me." He raised stricken eyes to Brian.

The kid wasn't lying about his feelings for Jodi Wilson. The pain on his face was raw and real.

"Did you take the gun with you?" Brian pressed on.

"I don't think so."

"You don't know?"

'I can't remember. But I never saw it again."

"Where did you and Jodi go?"

"We went to the diner." He ducked his eyes. "I eat when I get high. Then Jodi convinced me to go back and help Jake. The buzz was wearing off and she got through to me. Jake was gone when we got back to the trailer. If it wasn't for the blood soaked rug I would have sworn it was a bad trip and never happened. We looked all over for him. Never saw Jake again." His eyes were wild, crazed.

"Where was the rug when we searched the trailer the first time?"

"I put it in a plastic bag and drove to a pond on my bike. It's a shit hole for waste run-off. Nobody goes there. I dumped it under a big rock. Was going to leave it there..."

"Why didn't you?"

Grief-stricken eyes bored through Brian. "I went back and got it when we decided to move. Scrubbed it with bleach. She made it." Tears tracked his cheeks. "Jodi gave it to me for my birthday."

"Sloppy, huh, Ben?" Against Brian's will, he was inclined to believe him. "Why didn't you confess all this the first time you were questioned?"

"I was fucking scared. And I *didn't* know where Jake went. This is all a fucking nightmare." His head hung in his hands again and Brian had had enough.

Swinging a leg clear, he sprung off the chair, its wooden legs grating against the linoleum floor. Knuckles on the table Brian fired at Ben, "That's not the way it happened, is it, Ben? You shot Jake in the leg and he laughed, all right. He taunted you, didn't he? Maybe even dared you to shoot him again. And Jodi pleaded with you to stop, but you put a bullet in Jake's brain, didn't you?"

Ben wagged his head in denial.

Brian's accusations kept coming, "You put a bullet in his brain and then stuffed him in a sleeping bag and drove for hours to get rid of his body. And Jodi helped you. Because she loved you, she helped you. And couldn't live with it and threatened to confess. But you couldn't let her do that, could you, Ben? You had to kill her, too, and stop her from talking."

"No! No! No!" Hysterical, snot streamed out of Ben's nose, tears poured down his face. "It didn't happen that way. How could I get rid of Jake's body? I don't even own a *car*, man!" Ben shouted. "I loved Jodi," he blubbered. "I didn't, I didn't...."

Out of steam, Brian's chest heaved. *Son of a bitch. The kid's telling the truth.* Brian stalked away from the table, reversed direction and strode back. He turned the recorder off.

"Fuck." Brian glanced at Joe who still leaned against the wall, his face composed, a penetrating gleam in his eye. He nodded twice.

Damn it. Joe believes him, too. Brian's heart ached with regret. How could he believe this low-life punk so easily and not have believed Matty? *Forgive me, sweetheart.*

A couple raps on the door brought Brian over to it. A uniformed officer stood on the other side, his features blurred through the glass panel. Brian opened the door, hung his head out.

"You done with him?"

"Yeah, for the time being." Brian swung the door open for the officer.

Joe pushed himself away from the tobacco stained, beige wall. The officer handcuffed Ben and nudged him towards the door.

Ben twisted around to see Brian. "You believe me?"

"Mostly."

Ben's eyes lit. "Then you'll help me?"

"No promises. I'll see what I can do."

Brian and Joe grabbed their jackets and trailed Ben out of the room. Outside a cool wind whipped the ends of Brian's hair and chilled his sweat-soaked shirt, but not enough to make him want to put his coat on. "Damn it was hot in there. Thanks for having my back, Joe."

"Hey, it's what we Sullivans do. Can you drop me at the house? Bobbie needed my car today. Hers is in the shop."

"No problem." Brian drove back to the suburbs, lost in thought, the radio substituting for conversation.

Taking the exit ramp nearest Joe's house Brian mentioned, "Guess we have to start all over. Caprisi will have my badge or at least demote me."

Brian braked in front of Joe's house, the line of solar lanterns leading to the front door a welcoming, homey glow in the darkness.

"Go home. Get a good night's sleep," Joe counseled. "We'll figure it out tomorrow." Half of Joe's body jutted out of Brian's car, his brother obviously eager to see his family. Brian swallowed his envy.

"Thanks for everything, Joe."

"No problem. Do you want to come in for a beer?"

"Not tonight. See you in the morning."

Brian waited on line at the local drive through for a couple of burgers and fries and drove slowly home. Dark windows greeted him. No lights shining, no one waiting for his return. His home had never been more than a place to unwind after a stressful workday, but he had never been lonely before at his homecomings. Until now.

Flicking on the lights and closing his front door, he ambled over to the TV and switched it on for background noise, a frequent habit. He missed Matty and needed to speak with her, apologize and clear the air. Maybe convince her to grab a late dinner with him somewhere. Punching in her number on his cell phone he sat on the couch shrill rings in his ear. No answer and another frustrating trip to her voicemail recording. He hung up without leaving a message.

Tomorrow he'd restart the search for Jake's killer. But first he would make things right with Matty, even if he had to camp out in her clinic parking lot to do it.

Chapter 14

Rearranging files and pushing papers around her desk didn't distract Matilda enough. Her cheeks still burned, dwelling on the mortifying situation yesterday morning. The embarrassing repercussions of her impulsive behavior stung stubbornly and the string of "shouldn't haves" marched through her mind in depressing repetitions—shouldn't have gone to the police station without setting an appointment with Brian first and/or attended the meeting with the Whitmans in the first place—shouldn't have imparted contradictory information about an investigation in front of the victim's parents or taken her dismissal from the case personally. Probably shouldn't have avoided Brian's phone calls, either. How many were there? Maybe eight. Obviously, he wanted to connect with her.

For what purpose? Castigate her for sabotaging the case against Ben? Rub in the fiasco after she had given him her truth about the hidden gun? Impossible to reconcile the frosty and obstinate homicide detective with the passionate, poetic man who made love to her like she was the only woman on earth. And for her, he was the only man. Better to avoid him until she could analyze her flyaway thoughts and calm her rioting spirit.

Although she'd yet to tell him, she had already forgiven Brian for his officious behavior having faced similar responses by "men in blue" before. Eventually truth had prevailed in investigations she'd been party to in the past and Matilda remained confident the Jake Ashford case would be no exception. But she had never been in love with a policeman before and that twist was one mighty big exception. For her to envision a future loving Brian, he had to love her enough now to believe her. Since he hadn't told her he loved her and he didn't believe her either, where the hell did that leave them?

Oh, but the sheer wonder of making love with him. The tantalizing mental picture of Brian arching above her on the bed, gloriously naked, muscles tensed, wanting her with his eyes, his hands, his gorgeous body, persisted in 3-D Technicolor far more pervasively than any of her truths ever had—or ever would, she conceded.

Was it too early to respond to his multiple voicemail requests and call him back now? Matilda glanced at her watch. Barely five-thirty. Not yet.

The back entrance bell chimed with its xylophonic ding-dong rousing Clyde from a dead sleep on his spot on the floor where the first tentative rays of dawn streaked his coat. His ears pricked and he raised his head sniffing the air. A growl rumbled in his throat, escalated to a full bark as he sprang up and lunged toward the shadow of a man looming through her open office door.

At first delighted, assuming Shamus was early to work, too, Matilda became perplexed at Clyde's watchdog reaction and the subsequent transformation of the shadow into James Whitman on a tear into her office. Panting he rushed toward her desk wild-eyed and shouting, "Hurry! Please! Max was hit by a car! Please!"

Clyde looped circles around the man barking in throaty whoops, his nails scratching the wood floor. "What?" Matilda rose from her chair rapidly, grabbed the handle of her doctor bag and rounded her desk toward Mr. Whitman in a split second.

He reversed and she followed, delivering the order, "Clyde heel," in a firm voice. Matilda passed through the office door, paused and commanded. "Stay." She pulled the door closed behind her.

"Where is he?" she called out to Mr. Whitman's back as he rushed down the hall ahead of her.

"Out back in my SUV," came his response in muffled, breathy bursts. "You've got to put him out, doc. He's bleeding and howling like he's *screaming*." He broke gait to glimpse at her over his shoulder, "It's awful."

Following Whitman's retreat toward the back door she requested, "Hold on a second, let me get something for him." Matilda ducked into the pharmacy alcove and rummaged in the cabinet for a vial of anesthesia, a syringe, a roll of gauze, while Mr. Whitman waited, one leather-gloved hand on the back door knob.

"I've never heard a dog scream...horrible." He pinched his brow with two fingers.

Clutching the vial and needle in one hand, she ran through the door Mr. Whitman flung open. Adrenaline coursing through her body, Matilda pounded down the steps, ran at top speed toward the car, rear door gaping open above the roofline of the SUV.

"Lexxie will never forgive me. In the back of the car, doctor. Hurry!"

Only the crunching sound of gravel dislodged under her flying feet, no distant traffic noise, no chirping birds and no howling dog.

Please don't let me be too late.

Sprinting along the driver side of the car, she turned with a lunge to round the rear bumper. She ground to a halt, half falling into the trunk area. Breath ragged in her throat, she dropped her bag and medical supplies in one corner. Her hands free to tend to Max, she leaned in. She stared at the empty cargo space. Her palms spread on a plastic tarp, her mind wheeling to comprehend. She twisted her head to one side in the direction of Mr. Whitman's heavy breathing. "Where's..."

A hinge squeaked, the light in the trunk

darkened instantaneously. A dull thwack shot an explosion of pain across her back, ramming her face into the smothering, oily plastic. The unremitting pressure of the rear door pinned her half inside the car, her legs dangling outside. With effort she tamped the cloying plastic away from her nostrils with her hands and was able to swivel her head. With one cheek crushed against the tarp, she fought to reclaim her breath. The trunk door released with a whoosh of air in her face, then out of one eye, a brief glimpse of an arm swinging above her head. "Stop, don't..." she gasped weakly, her lungs on fire. Devoid of the strength to raise her hand against the coming blow, the rock in his hand struck her head with stunning force. Pain rocketed into her skull with the impact to her ear like a thunderclap of agony. Groaning, she plummeted into inky blackness.

****

Hey. Thanks. It shouldn't have come to this, you know? Hell, it's only money. I'm sorry I pressed so hard. But man, a shot in the leg is nothing if I don't settle this score. I'm bleeding here. Just help me now, all right?

Jake sprawled on the floor of the trailer propped up on both elbows with upturned eyes, seemingly relaxed despite his injury, a half smile on his face. His chest bare, blood spotted the white shirt tied like a tourniquet above one knee, the foot propped on the seat of a dilapidated kitchen chair. His smile froze and then vanished, eyes narrowing. "What are you doing?" He kicked his leg off the chair and dove into a prone position, his stomach partially off a bloodied throw rug. Palms flattened on the floor, elbows pointed up, he flexed his arms into a pushup and gained purchase with one foot on the floor attempting to stand on one leg.

The barrel of a pistol came into view pointing at the back of Jake's head. Now the full gun, gloved finger on the trigger, an arm in a leather sleeve. The gun pressed against the back of Jake's skull. The jacket shoulder—a face. James Whitman's face, hatred shimmering in diabolical eyes. A shot!

Matilda came back to a reality more unreal than the movie reel in her head. Tumbling and pitching in the back of the lurching car, she hit the bruised side of her head against the seat back. Vomit rose in her throat, a burning acid. She gulped, engaging her gag reflex, as her body tossed around the cargo area like a bouncing ball. Ears ringing, vision blurry, she strained to anchor herself on the rolling sea of motion. With one outstretched arm against the side of the car, she peered through the seat separation of the front seat and spied the back of Whitman's head above the driver's seat. Her hand investigated a warm stream trickling down her neck, seeping from her ear. Blood pooled in the cavity of her ear, sticky on her fingers. Sliding her hand beneath the plastic under her, she wiped her fingers on the car rug, leaving some DNA behind.

Branches cracked and splintered, grating against both sides of the SUV. If she could drag her way to the cargo door she might open it, throw herself out of the moving car. Anything was better than continuing this imprisonment with Jake's killer. And Jodi Wilson's, too. *At least I can still think. I've got to get out of here. Please Lord.*

Each inch of progress came undone by the pitching movement of the car. One upward lurch had her biting her tongue on the downturn, blood salty on her mouth, conking her already unbearably sore head on the floor. The car lurched to a halt, a door opened. Scrambling in an attempt to sit up, the plastic tarp crackled and slid under her body, flattening her on the floor, impeding her escape. She reached a hand behind her and pulled the lever to unlatch the seat. Twisting, she dove at it, folding it down, and flung her body into the other back seat. A searing pain nearly tore her apart on impact with the car seat as the cargo door swung up and open.

"Shit!" he bellowed.

Frantic, she threw open her door and pitched out—unsteady but her legs held. In a terror-infused state, she hobbled, desperate to flee—her heart hammered and tears streamed—every scrap of will impelling, driving her jogger's body into a run to escape this murderer.

Too late.

He plowed into her from behind, the tackle bouncing her chin on the forest floor, filling her mouth with leaves. She spit them out and winced as he yanked her arms behind her and wound rope around her crisscrossed wrists. Breasts pressed against the hard ground, her heart pounded a drumbeat on the dirt. His fingers clenched the suit jacket material between Matty's shoulder blades and tugged her upright with a breath-robbing, forward shove. "Move!"

Standing now, she sucked in a lungful of air and screamed, "Help! Help me!"

Another shove delivered to the small of her back jettisoned her forward.

"Oomph..." Staggering, the wind knocked out of her, she barely managed to keep from falling on her face again.

"Scream your brains out—nobody will hear you."

Why's that? Stumbling forward his footfalls behind her, she scanned the area for something, anything familiar. *There has to be a way out of this. Shit, my phone's in the office. Where's my doctor's bag, the syringe? I could pump him full of the Versed.*

Matilda stopped, dared to turn around and confront him, "Why are you doing this? Where are you taking me?"

He gestured with an impatient thrust of his arm, "Turn around and keep walking." The hypodermic needle poked out of the web of his glove.

Dear God.

The nightmare procession continued through a serene landscape of angled sunrays that striped the tree trunks, skittering crackles from unseen creatures and the occasional plunk of acorns landing on the ground. Her head cleared, all her senses heightened acutely and primed to create an opportunity to live through this somehow. Matilda eyed the forest floor, spied heavy branches, scattered rocks. Without the use of her hands, she couldn't fathom a way to arm herself and attack her attacker.

Mist blanketed the ground thirty feet ahead of her, partially obscuring the tree trunks and swirling upward into the sparse canopy of leaves with wispy wakes like vaporous tails. Advancing into the fog, she trod on damper leaves, the ground slick with mud. The air smelled pungent, sour like stagnant water and mold. Cottony air enveloped her, bound and limping in a cloud, the most otherworldly experience in her life. She had never thought to *send* a message before, had no idea if she could transmit telepathically. *Grandma Pearl, Shamus, somebody hear me. I'm in danger.*

The mist thinned, dissolved and she broke into a clearing. Two steps and her feet planted on the Prairie Path. The stone bridge that overlooked Whitman's hiding place for Jake's body lay up ahead, apparently his intended destination for Matilda Connors' body, too

Rough hands grasped her wrists and wrenched her to a stop on the center of the bridge. Matilda spun around moving out of arm's reach from him, buying time. "Why are we here? It's the first place they'll look if you kill me."

Whitman smirked. His remorseless eyes speared her and rocketed icy shivers through her veins, her body shaking so hard her teeth chattered. "Maybe. But with you gone nobody can tie me to his body, no less yours."

She glimpsed at the swirling water below out of the corner of her eye and considered her options. First she'd have to hurdle the stone railing and then swim with her hands tied behind her back. *Keep him talking.* "I didn't know you killed Jake until today. I may never have known if you hadn't done this."

He shrugged, "Couldn't take that chance. By the way, how the hell did you know where he was? You are one crazy bitch."

She trained accusing eyes on Whitman. "How could you kill your own son?"

"That's rich—*my* son," he sneered. "I've wanted to kill that no-good bastard for years. Surely you knew that with your magic crystal ball." He assessed her, dead-eyed. "The bum broke his mother's heart. But still she adored him. Right or wrong, she always took his side. She would choose him over me in a heartbeat. So I gave her no choice." Whitman studied the syringe in his hand, gave her a lazy emotionless glance, like he had all the time in the world to execute her in the early morning solitude. "The drugs should have killed the little shit. Or at least the drug dealers. But no. The little weasel was charmed. Always managed to wrap my Alexis around his little finger."

He pulled the vial of Versed out of his jacket pocket with his free hand, held it loosely in his glove. "She'd do nothing to stop the inheritance on his twenty-first birthday. Didn't matter what I said, what *I* wanted for us. Ironic that his best buddy handed me the gun." He laughed, an evil cackle that horrified Matilda. "Another worthless piece of shit he is. He deserves to rot in jail."

Jabbing the needle into the vial, he pulled the plunger back slowly, the liquid sucking into the chamber, filling it.

Matilda flexed her knocking knees preparing to put adrenaline to use and leap onto the narrow ledge rimming the bridge. *Dear God in heaven, save me.*

She took a deep breath as James Whitman sprang forward, the needle a sword aimed at her.

Chapter 15

Brian shot his arm out from under the blanket. He groped to pound the snooze button on the alarm clock buzzing near his ear, like a dental drill on steroids. He pounded air. Disoriented and blurry eyed, he sat up. *Where the hell am I?*

Shifting his hips, one leg slid off the leather couch in his living room, his back stiff and achy. The television cast shadows in the room and the annoying drilling sound continued from his cell phone vibrating a dance along the top of the coffee table.

He grabbed it and grunted, "Yeah, Sullivan."

"Detective Sullivan. I'm sorry to bother you so early. I never expected you to answer. I was planning on leaving a voice mail. This is Lexxie Whitman, Jake's mom."

"No bother, I was up." Brian didn't have the heart to tell her otherwise. "What can I do for you, Mrs. Whitman?"

"I planned a memorial service today for Jake. The coroner released his body last night. He said I would need to contact you to have his personal effects returned. I hoped he was wearing his St. Christopher's medal when you found him. You mentioned a medal…"

Soft sobbing wrenched his heart and he delayed a few seconds before answering, "Yes ma'am, I can bring you the medal."

She sniffed. "It was his dad's and I would like him to have it."

"I understand. I'll leave here as soon as I can and make the arrangements to release your son's personal things. I'll drop it off at your home."

"I would appreciate it. Thank you so much. I hate being a nuisance."

"You are not a nuisance. What time is the service, ma'am? My brother and I would like to come."

"At two PM at the Morton Arboretum." Her voice cracked and her breathing caught on little whimpers. "Jake wasn't religious. It's a beautiful, peaceful place and I think he'd like his life celebrated there."

"We'll try to be there. I'll call you to verify that I have his personal effects to deliver."

"Thank you, Detective Sullivan."

Brian snapped the phone shut, dug around in the couch cushions until he found the remote control and turned off the television. He stretched his arms over his head, rubbed his hands over his face, stood and plodded into the kitchen still in a half-awake stupor. A quick flip of the switch on his coffee maker and coffee beans ground with a whiny uproar.

The light on the microwave digital display flashed repeatedly. He shook his head in disgust. *Damn I miss Jimmy. He knew how to fix that damn clock.* He flipped his cell phone open to check the time and groaned. *Four thirty? It's still night.*

In the bathroom he splashed his face with cold water, brushed his teeth and tossed his wrinkled shirt in the hamper. Clad in a starched, blue-pinstriped white shirt, a navy tie, and gray slacks with a dark gray sport coat over his arm, he was halfway ready for the day. *Caffeine and I'll be good to go.*

Brian filled his travel mug and drank a couple gulps of coffee. He ignored his burning tongue and throat needing the caffeine jolt more. Draining the cup, he refilled it. His mind clearing, the pre-dawn wake-up call provided the opportunity to check for Jake's medal and clear out before facing his boss.

Caprisi would not take the news about Jarvis' innocence well, an understatement. *Hopefully I'll still have a job when the tongue-lashing is over.*

Smiling wryly, he anticipated Matty's tongue-lashing, too. Last time he begged her forgiveness had ended far beyond his wildest expectations. *Matty.* He hoped she'd let him silence her with kisses—for hours.

****

The jeep engine rumbled overloud through the quiet suburban neighborhoods, a few joggers and paper deliverymen his only companions on the roads leading to the Whitman home. A small, gray, cardboard box perched on the passenger seat. *That's it. That's all that Jake Ashford left for his mom.*

It didn't matter anymore that he had argued with his mother, that he had made bad decisions and paid the price. The kid that sang happy birthday to his mom year after year was gone. Brian's work in homicide proved the fleeting nature of life on a daily basis, but the Jake Ashford case drove home "life's short" like a spike in Brian's gut.

The need to be with Matty, love her, and please, God, be loved, pressed on Brian with heart-racing urgency. Nothing else mattered, not his job, not her truths. Nothing was worth another day of separation from her. He would make it right today.

Brian pulled up at the security gate. A bored, half-asleep guard noted Brian's upheld badge and waved him through. Grabbing the box off the seat he left the car, closing the door softly, and strode down the blue stone walkway leading to the Whitman's front door, his booming footsteps thudding in the stillness of the morning. The door was cracked open. Brian unsnapped his gun.

"Mrs. Whitman? Hello." He peered inside with one eye, his body angled to the left of the doorframe and detected movement.

Mrs. Whitman swung the door open. "Sorry,

Detective. I was carrying things out to the garbage when I saw your car at the entrance so I left it open for you." She blew on a section of hair that had escaped from a clasp on top of her head.

Brian offered, "Can I help you carry anything?"

"No, thank you. It gives me something to do. Helps me keep my mind off ..." She paused, held her chest and breathed deeply. "As if there will be one second of the rest of my life that I will not remember my baby."

Helpless sympathy for the woman pierced Brian as tears streamed down her face.

"May I come in?"

She answered with a shaky nod.

Gently cupping her shoulders he steered her backward, clear of the arc of the door as he closed it.

She drew a wadded tissue from her pocket and swiped away tears. "Come sit down. Can I get you anything? Coffee? Tea?"

"Nothing, thank you." He followed her into the sunroom at the rear of the house, placed the cardboard box on the coffee table and sat in a hard, uncomfortable chair.

Rummaging in the box, she picked out the holy medal and clasped it to her heart. "I can't thank you enough for bringing the medal to me. It means everything to be able to give it back to Jake today." Her shadowed gray eyes stared at him. Brian recognized the lost hollowness there, the same cast in his mother's eyes since Jimmy's murder. A mother should never have to live through the pain of burying her child.

"I questioned Ben Jarvis again yesterday after our meeting. I'm convinced he didn't kill Jake."

Expecting outrage, Brian was surprised by her calm thoughtful demeanor. "So Matty Connors is right."

Guilt sliced through him. "Yes, ma'am, I believe that's true. I will do everything in my power to find who shot Jake. I will not let his killer go free."

"I know you will and I thank you. I'm relieved that it wasn't Ben. Ben was like a son to me. He even brought his girlfriend here wanting our approval. We both told Ben that she seemed like such a nice girl who made him happy." She paused, eyes closed. When she gazed at him again, her tears glistened. "The boys were always so close. Ben practically lived here when Jake was little. Their fascination with model trains was such a bond, even as teenagers."

On an intake of held breath, Brian's pulse raced. "Trains?"

"Nowadays kids have video games, but Jake and Ben collected trains. They spent hours building tracks. I liked knowing where they were and what they were doing. I am almost finished boxing up Jake's set in the basement. I was going to throw them out but I think I'll hold on to them. If Ben straightens out his life he might appreciate having them." She shook her head. "I'm sorry to go on like that." Standing, apparently through reminiscing, she said, "Thank you again for bringing Jake's things."

"Your welcome. If there is anything else I can do for you, please, just call. Don't leave your door open. You really should keep it closed and locked. I don't want to alarm you, but Jake's killer is still at large."

The gun was *in the boxcar*. Brian hesitated following her to the door. "Mind if I have a look at those trains?"

Facing him she widened her eyes, tipped her head in a curious expression. After a couple headshakes, she replied, "I don't mind." She headed toward a door at the back of the stairway. "They're down here."

Brian clumped down the stairs behind her. He squatted and sorted through the box she indicated for a few minutes before extracting a boxcar with a six-inch sliding door. "*It was blue with white letters on one side. It had two larger letters, like a logo, on the other side. A 'B' and an 'M'...*"

Holding the car matching Matty's description in his hand, Brian sprang up from a squat, modulating his voice to casually ask, "Where's your husband, Mrs. Whitman?"

"Out for a morning jog. Why?"

Brian set the boxcar back in the box. "Will you please ask him to call me when he returns?" He handed her his business card. "I'd like to speak with him."

She pocketed the card, brows pinched. "Of course."

Mind reeling, Brian bounded up to the first floor, turned and waited for her to mount the steps. He hurried to the door, anxious to call in the APB on Whitman.

"James should be back any minute and I'll keep the door locked from now on. Thank you for caring."

"No problem, ma'am."

Sprinting to the car, Brian dove in making a grab for the radio mic and called in the APB. He slammed the car door shut and hit the gas, whizzing past the guard station at sixty mph. Careening at top speed over snaking roads, he blasted onto Roosevelt Road for the five mile, straight shot, bound toward the connecting street that fronted Matty's house. Eyes directed straight ahead, he positioned his cell phone in front of his face and dialed her number.

Shit. No answer. Maybe she's still sleeping.

No choice but voicemail. "Matty. I'm five minutes from your house. Do *not* open your door for anyone but me. Whitman killed Jake and I don't know his whereabouts. I'll be right there."

Screeching to a halt in front of her house, he leaped out of the car, raced up the steps and pounded on the door with no response.

Penny emerged from the neighboring front door, tugging a big, black dog over the threshold by inches, her boy in tow. "Quit banging, Brian! She isn't home!" she hollered.

Dropping his fist to his side, he descended the steps and met Penny in her driveway still tugging the recalcitrant mutt. "Did you see her leave? It's too early for her to be working, isn't it?"

"I heard her car start up a little after five. Thin walls around here." She glared at the dog. "Move, Moose. I mean it."

Owen wore a pained expression and Moose held his ground.

"I'm sure she's at the clinic now." Penny leaned her whole body into reining on the dog leash, a scant couple inches progress her reward. "We have a seven-thirty appointment for Moose with her so I can still get to work in time. Come on, Moose!" She yanked on the leash. "He hates going to the v-e-t, but even if I spell the dumb dog somehow knows the score."

"Let me help you. You're going to hurt yourself."

Brian winked at Owen, who grinned at him—*the cutest kid*. Hoisting Moose easily into submission, he hauled the sixty-pound dog to Penny's car and placed him in the backseat.

"Don't be a sissy, Moose. Dr. Matty isn't going to hurt you, is she, Owen?" Brian stroked the quivering dog's head.

"Stop, don't..." Matty gasped, sprawled on a plastic tarp half-in the car trunk, her head sideways, her eye wild. Whitman struck her head with a rock. She groaned, her eye closed. He shoved her legs inside and slammed the door shut.

"Oh my God, Matty! Where are you?" Brian yelled.

The dog barked, rearing his head beneath Brian's hands.

"Brian, you're scaring Owen," Penny

admonished him.

"Why are you doing this? Where are you taking me?"

"I hear you, Matty. Tell me where you are." Brian stared downward, unseeing—the jerky movements of the dog's furry body nothing but a blur.

"Jake's bridge."

"I'm coming, Matty. Hold on." Brian's heart pounded in his chest. Light-headed, he uttered, "Sorry. I have to go."

Brian shut the back door.

"Is everything all right Brian?" Penny yelled out the window.

"Police business."

He sprinted to his car, his cell phone to his ear.

Joe answered on the first ring.

"Whitman has Matty on the bridge where she found Jake. She's in trouble."

Brian ignored the blaring horn as he cut around a van idling at a red light, barely missing a truck in the intersection.

"What do you mean *has* her on the bridge?"

"I don't know." *Dear God, don't let her be in the water like Jake.* "Meet me there with backup." Hand on the horn, the speedometer needle inched towards seventy.

"How do you know she's in trouble?"

"No time to explain. Call an ambulance, too. Just trust me." He dropped the phone on the passenger seat as he barreled around a corner without braking. The jeep veered on two wheels, threatening to tip over counter clockwise. Brian pitched his body to the right and the far wheels touched ground, tires squealing. Pedal to the floor he drove the car off road, plunging onto the dirt path with bone-jarring impact.

He asked Joe for blind trust, just like Matty had asked for his.

Please, Matty, hold on. I'm coming. I'm almost there.

He couldn't lose her, wouldn't permit it. *She has to be OK. She will be. I'll stop him.*

Riding the jeep like a bucking horse, Brian spied two figures struggling up ahead on the bridge. Police sirens wailed in the distance, coming closer. *Thanks Joe!*

Slamming on the brakes, Brian rammed the shift into park and leaped out, gun drawn.

"Police!" he yelled on a run into the clearing, his arms straight out ahead of him, the nine millimeter leveled at Whitman's head.

James Whitman released Matty. She slithered against the stone bridge, collapsing on the ground.

Whitman planted his hands on the edge of the bridge and swung one leg up, the instep of his right shoe on the ledge.

"Stop or I'll shoot."

Whitman flexed his arms and his left leg moved inches off the ground. Brian took aim and shot him in the leg as he hurtled the railing.

Car doors slammed, a loud splash sounded. Brian raced to Matty.

Joe, followed by most of the homicide department, charged toward him. "I'm on him." The squad tailed Joe off path down the riverbank.

Matty slumped on her side, a syringe stuck in her arm. Brian kneeled, pulled the needle out, laid it on the ground and cradled her head in his shaking hands. Turning her gently, he sawed off the rope binding her wrists with his pocketknife, eased her body back down.

"Matty, can you hear me?"

Limp, her breathing shallow, her closed eyes fluttered.

"What was in the syringe? Please love, don't leave me." Tears welled in his eyes as he sat heavily on the ground and gathered her upper body into his lap. I need you."

Her lips opened slightly in an overbite emitting a tiny sound, "Vuh." She drew a ragged breath and rumbled, "Rrr."

She sagged in his embrace. "Stay with me, Matty, please."

Joe's head appeared at eye level, the rest of his body in degrees as he climbed the riverbank. Two uniformed cops dragged Whitman up between them.

As Joe knelt beside him, Brian exploded with frustration, "Did you call an ambulance? Where the hell is it?"

"It's on its way."

"We can't wait. Hold her a sec." Matty gasped as Brian lifted her into Joe's waiting arms, every subsequent breath too slow, like low groans.

Brian stood, positioned his arms below Joe's and lifted Matty gently.

"Let's go. I'll drive." Joe grabbed the syringe off the ground and sprinted, dripping wet to the squad car.

Hating that he jostled her so much as he sped toward the car, Joe helped him position her on his lap lengthwise on her side in the back seat. He wrapped her in his arms, pressing her chest against his, cradling her head on his shoulder to shield her from the relentless bumps from off-road driving.

Joe at the wheel, the car careened onto the asphalt road into traffic. The siren blared and Joe picked up a police escort on the race to the hospital.

Joe grabbed the radiophone and barked, "Lieutenant Joe Sullivan en route in squad car to Regional Trauma Center. Unknown injection. Victim unconscious. ETA six minutes. Who's the attending?"

"Doctor Molly Sullivan, officer."

"Good." Joe hung up.

Brian prayed over Matty's inanimate body, sick with fear during the longest six minutes of his life.

As Joe rocketed the car into the ambulance bay Brian caught sight of Molly standing outside the door with her team alongside a stretcher. For the first time since this nightmare began, Brian had a glimmer of hope.

Molly yanked the back door open and leaned inside with a member of her team, four outstretched arms accepting his Matty from him. "Oh, Brian," she exclaimed, her eyes kind. "Don't worry, we've got her."

With magical efficiency, Matty was placed on the stretcher and the medical team wheeled it through the door. Brian and Joe couldn't keep up on a full run. Inside, Joe handed the syringe to a nurse and then stood at Brian's side as Matty disappeared behind the emergency room doors.

"She can't die, Joe. She can't die."

Joe's soaking wet arm around his shoulder, Brian let his brother lead him to a molded-plastic waiting room chair.

Joe smiled at the admitting nurse who handed him a blanket. "Thanks."

He rubbed his clothes with the blanket and then draped it over his shoulders.

Brian clasped his hands in prayer, bent his head and closed his eyes. *Please, dear Lord, don't take her.*

When Brian opened his eyes, Joe's hands were prayer clasped, too.

Chapter 16

Crazed and desperate to rewind the past twenty-four hours, Brian drummed his heels on the floor, bobbling his thighs against his elbows. His sweat-soaked shirt, nearly as wet as his brother's, stuck to his chest and underarms. Chilly rivers of perspiration dripped down his face and back.

"Jesus, Joe, I don't know what the son of a bitch put in her!" Brian stared at the doors leading to the trauma rooms helpless, useless. "She was barely breathing." Brian cupped his face with his hands.

"I know." Joe's hand brushed his elbow. "Molly's with her. Focus on that."

Brian dipped his hand in his jacket pocket for his phone to *do* something—*anything* normal and productive in the surreal hell of waiting. "I suppose I should call her brother."

The inner doors opened and a trim woman in mint green scrubs hustled through them, stopped and called out, "Brian Sullivan!"

"Yes, uh here." Brian raised an arm as he stood.

"I'll call the brother," Joe offered.

"Shamus Connors. Lives over the animal clinic."

Joe nodded.

"Thanks, Joe." Brian advanced toward the lady in green.

"I'm Trudy Howard, Dr. Sullivan's physician's assistant. She wants to speak with you," she said rapid-fire, and then directed, "Follow me."

Pivoting neatly in an athletic half-spin, she power-walked back through the doors.

Tracking her rapid movements in the brightly lit corridor that glowed sterile white, pungent antiseptic and sickness smells heightened the surreal. *I put her here. I led Whitman to her and this is my fault.* Brian's stomach pitched with the rush of self-disgust. Then his heart froze like a rock in his chest when he turned into the trauma room several paces behind Trudy and witnessed the cold hard truth of Matty's condition.

"She's arresting," came Molly's soft voice followed by a flurry of activity around the devices, tubes, wires that surrounded Matty. "Paddles."

The invasive medical equipment struck Brian as an affront to Matty's delicate breasts, the lacy beige bra. She had a ventilator tube in her mouth and Brian had to close his eyes to temporarily blot out the images.

"Clear." The machine punched out a metallic crack. Another whined an eerie squeal.

"Again. Clear," Molly demanded.

The same mechanical punch sounded followed by sonar-like blips. "Sinus."

Brian opened his eyes. Relief flooded as Molly handed over the paddles to Trudy and turned toward him, her eyes serious over her surgical mask, the consummate professional.

She pulled the mask down beneath her chin. "Bri, fast, was she conscious when you reached her?"

"Yes." Brian's heart raced, intent on providing critical information that might save her, but how? He had nothing.

"Did you ask her what was in the syringe?"

"Yes, but she couldn't talk, just a couple syllables. Joe brought the syringe. Can't you test it?"

"No time. What did she try to say? Think!"

Brian wracked his brain. "She made a motion like biting her lip. A 'vuh' sound. Then she garbled like 'grr'."

Molly's gaze shifted down, seconds passed in silence. "Are you sure she made a G sound the second time? Could it have been just Rs?"

"Uh, yes. Yes, it could."

Molly wheeled around. "Start 2mg Romazicon. Bri, I'll send someone out to the waiting room when we have her stabilized."

Understanding the dismissal, Brian still was torn. Equally reluctant to leave Matty or stay, a helpless witness to her suffering, he trudged back out to the waiting room and sat next to Joe.

"How's it going in there?"

"Touch and go. She went into cardiac arrest when I got to her room." Tears welled. "They brought her back. Molly said they'd get her stabilized. I have to believe that, Joe, or I'll go nuts."

"Hey," Joe remarked, smiling at him for the first time that morning, "If Molly Sullivan says she can fix somebody, they're fixed. Want a cup of coffee or something?"

"Nah. I'm already too wired."

"OK. Then tell me why the hell Whitman attacked her and while you're at it, how the hell you knew where she was."

Brian chuckled. "Whitman killed Jake. And Jodi Wilson."

Joe's eye widened, shocked. "You're fucking kidding me. How'd you pull that out of your ass?"

"I brought Jake's personal effects to Alexis Ashford-Whitman this morning, a medal for his funeral service and she mentioned model trains. Long story, but the missing boxcar?"

Joe nodded.

"In the basement."

"So *you* called in the APB on Whitman. Caught it on the scanner."

"Right. And then I hightailed it over to Matty's house. She wasn't there. Whitman already had her."

"How'd you know?"

"I saw it. And then I heard her." Brian shrugged his shoulders, eyes rounded as if he couldn't believe it either.

"Caprisi's going to give you a medal." Joe stood, tapped Brian on the shoulder. "I better move my car out of the ambulance bay and get to work. I'll enjoy calling the D.A. and processing Whitman."

"Could be tricky. I don't have all the pieces yet. Would be nice if we can wring a confession out of him, let him finish the puzzle for us."

"They brought him in for the bullet wound while you were back there. I'll let the uniforms bring him to the station house."

"Poor Mrs. Whitman." Pity stabbed Brian. *The service this afternoon on the heels of the official police notification that her husband is being held for murdering her son.* "Maybe you could figure the most...sensitive way to tell her?"

"Damned if I know how. But I'll handle it. I left messages for Shamus Connors at the clinic and at home. I'll swing by there first and tell him about Matty."

"Thanks, Joe." Brian rose off the chair, hand outstretched.

Joe swung an arm to clasp Brian's hand and pulled him into a muscular hug. The bracing contact strengthened Brian, assuaged the nagging worry that Matty might not pull through. Joe's hands dropped and he assessed Brian, that scrutinizing glare of his deep blue eye next to the stark black eye patch. "You going to be OK if I leave now?"

"If she's OK I will," Brian said weakly.

"All right. Talk to you later. Call me when she's out of the woods."

Joe turned toward the door and Brian sank into the seat, prepared to stare into space until the agonizing vigil ended. Joe hesitated halfway out the door and turned around.

"Do me a favor?" A smirk on his face, he waited.

"Hell, yeah. Anything," Brian vowed.

Joe returned to the seat next to Brian, hunched near and said in a low voice, "Marry the woman before you make her pregnant. I don't think Ma could live through another one like me."

Despite the emotional roller coaster he had ridden with Joe that day, they laughed.

"I'll keep that in mind," Brian promised, heavy on the sarcasm.

Joe clapped his shoulder and left the hospital. Back to bouncing his elbows against his thighs, Brian watched the clock on the waiting room wall, waiting for word on Matty. Regret pummeled him. *Why didn't I just believe her? How could I leave her unprotected?*

A half hour passed, then an hour. Brian's trepidation grew with each revolution of the second hand on the round clock. He didn't know how to interpret the passage of time. *Is this a good thing? Or is she fighting for her life?*

About to storm the trauma room and beg to at least hold her hand, Brian focused on the inner door and willed it to open and usher forth his sister-in-law with good news. When Molly appeared minutes later through the same door, minus the surgical gloves and mask, a pretty blonde in an immaculate white doctor's jacket, he took her visit to the waiting room as prayers answered. He sprang up and rushed toward her, "Is she OK?"

Molly's blue eyes warmed with her smile. She nodded, said the magical words, "She'll be fine."

"Thank God!" Brian scooped her up and held the tiny woman in a hug a foot off the ground.

Molly giggled. "Put me down. I want to talk to you."

He obliged, happy to grin back at her. "Can I see her now?"

"In a minute. Let's sit."

Molly steered him to the nearest chairs and he sat, transfixed on her face. "The drug injected into her was a benzodiazepine, most likely Versed. That would explain her 'vuh' sound and the successful reversal with Romazicon. The Versed is an anesthesia and overdose causes respiratory problems and cardiac arrest. Unfortunately she was highly overdosed. We have her on a ventilator and I admitted her. She's in a private room, just for overnight. She should be breathing on her own soon. I want her monitored here before I release her. We dosed the Romazicon slowly until she regained consciousness. It was fleeting. She's still basically under, but I'd describe it as sleep rather than coma. She's going to have a major headache and we'll help make her comfortable with pain medication. Maybe nausea and dizziness. She's concussed, has several broken ribs and deep tissue bruises. For sure she'll feel like shit...not much of a medical term, but it works. Bottom line. After some rest she'll be as good as new." She gave him a wan smile. "Do I want to know how this all happened?"

"No." Brian shook his head. "No, you don't. Just be glad you never worked a case with Danny."

"Oh, hell yeah. She's in room 410. Want me to take you?"

"I can find it. Thank you from the bottom of my heart, sis."

Molly's eyes gleamed with a sly, know-all, female glint. "Is there going to be another Sullivan wedding?"

Brian rolled his eyes. "You and Kay always get all jazzed up over weddings. Jeez, now Bobbie can gang up on me, too. See you later."

"Come on," Molly invited as she stood. "I'll walk with you to the elevator."

Heavy-hearted, Brian traversed more sterile, hospital-smelling corridors until he stopped in the doorway of room 410. Straight ahead, a row of six-inch strips of material hung on diagonal planes to the window that let angled sunlight into the otherwise dim room. Just a tiny bump in the taut white sheet at the foot of the mattress indicated that anyone occupied the bed. Bubbling liquid, sucking, clicking and whooshing sounds repeated rhythmically.

Brian took hesitant, halting steps into the room, peering around the end of a short inner wall to find her sleeping. Before he continued around the bed toward a side chair, he lingered, arched over her bed.

Her honey blonde hair fell away from her face, tangled and wild against the thin pillow. A large bruise stained the side of her face purple, greenish-black. Her full lips parted in an oval around a ridged tube that trailed over her neck and shoulders sideways and attached to the ventilator that sucked and whooshed with the rise and fall of her chest. Those luscious lips were split in two places; brownish-maroon strips of dried blood marring the mouth he hungered to cover with his to tenderly ease the soreness away.

Fury rose in his throat, a bitter taste on his tongue. He had no outlet in the hushed room; he wanted to punch Whitman senseless, punch the wall and break things. Sinking into the chair, he gazed at Matty, his love. Lifting her hand carefully to his lips, he turned it and kissed her palm, the sweet, soft skin banishing his bitterness until he noticed the abrasions and angry welts around her wrist from being bound by that bastard.

Brian clenched his jaw. *Is Whitman still around here somewhere? Maybe I should go find him.*

Matty gagged, a groaning sound reverberating in her throat.

Stroking her arm lightly above the IV needle site, Brian stared at her face. She squeezed the muscles of her upper face, grunted and then relaxed, her eyes unmoving beneath closed eyelids. "Matty, can you hear me? I'm here. I won't leave you. Do you hurt, sweetheart?"

****

Brian's voice soothed Matty's aching body and troubled spirit, convinced her to calm down and not battle the gagging, smothering thing in her throat.

Her nightmare slayer.

The nightmarish memory of captivity in that sinister man's truck, her inability to escape, his awful remorseless admissions of killing quit ruminating in her brain. Brian had heard her, saved her. *And he's with me now. I'll get through this.*

Oddly she couldn't seem to open her eyes, move at all. Rapid footfalls sounded, came nearer. She smelled baby powder and musky cologne.

"I didn't know you had a visitor, Matilda," a soprano voice said.

"Are you her husband?" a deep male voice asked.

"No. I'm Detective Sullivan. I brought her in."

"You shouldn't be in here," the man said sternly.

Brian's hand went away. Matilda ached to get rid of this thing in her mouth and tell these people to let him stay. "Uhhhhhh," she groaned.

"I won't leave her. Speak to ER Attending Molly Sullivan. She'll clear me."

"Pft, pft, pft." The cuff around her upper arm tightened and a cool hand pressed a cold disc at the crook of her arm. The cuff deflated. "Vitals are normal," a woman said.

Matilda gagged repetitively, choking. *Get this thing out!*

"Step out in the hall for a few minutes, detective. I'm taking her off the ventilator," the man ordered, the doctor, Matty assumed.

Brian's warm hand touched her arm again, so soothing. "I'll be right back, Matty."

"Matilda." The doctor's Scope-scented breath fanned her face. "I want you to try to take a deep breath on the count of three and then blow it out as hard as you can. Can you do that for me?"

She managed to grunt.

"Ready? One, two, three."

Matty did as directed and when she blew out an awful object snaked up her throat like her windpipe was yanked out of her mouth. After several terrible seconds, it was blessedly gone. Her throat raw, she breathed normally.

A light pat on her hand. "You're doing fine. Rest now."

Footsteps receded.

"Visiting hours don't start until noon, detective, except for family. You really need to let her rest," the doctor advised in muted tones from far away it seemed.

"Can I just stay a few more minutes, please? She's my girlfriend, doc."

Aw.

Heavy footfalls, a chair scraped on the floor. She breathed in and smelled Brian's shower soap, Irish Spring, and a tang of locker room aroma. His hand clenched hers and his other hand traced ticklish swirls up and down her arm.

"I'm back, sweetheart. They'll only let me stay a few more minutes so you can rest."

He kissed the back of her hand, held it to his face.

Dreamy and pain-free, Matty drifted. His voice pierced through the blankness, "I'm so very sorry, Matty. Please forgive me. I pray you will."

Now he wrapped both his hands around hers, a warm cocoon of pleasure from the simple connection. Of course, she forgave him. *I love you, Brian.*

"You were right about everything, Matty. I should have listened to you. I'm sorry. *The* Matty Connors has never been wrong. I found the train car. The one you saw. Blue with the same lettering. It was in the basement of the Whitman house. And the gun you saw in that boxcar was the gun Ben used to shoot Jake. Ben didn't put it there. James Whitman did. And Ben didn't kill Jake when he shot him. Jake must have called Whitman for help. Instead it appears Whitman went over, shot Jake in the head, then dumped his body. After that, he hid the gun downstairs. He used it to kill Jodi Wilson and left it at the scene to frame Ben. It had to have come down that way, although I don't know the whys of it. But I'm pretty sure about how it all happened. Matty, darling, I'm so sorry."

You're right about everything now, my love. And if I could open my eyes, I'd tell you why he did it.

Her hand lifted in his and brushed along the curve of his cheekbone. Her fingers moistened. *Don't cry, Brian. It's OK.*

"I'm going to go to work now, sweetheart. But I'll be back later. Rest."

The chair scraped again and the light beyond her closed eyelids darkened. His lips touched hers, feather light, a headier sensation than the drugs she must be on. "I will never hurt you again. I love you *the* Matty Connors. I love you, my Matty, with all my heart."

I love you, too, my Brian.

As the sound of his footsteps faded, she smiled.

Chapter 17

Matty, I need your help. I won't have time to say good-bye. Tell them all good-bye for me. Let them know how much I loved them. Tell her she was my world. She is going to need help going on with her life. She needs to follow her heart. Let her know I understand. Be her support. Thank you.

Matty jerked awake. *No. No. No.* Her arm reached out to reconnect with the solid, reassuring warmth of him, but the sheets lay tangled, cold next to her. Considering it best to have a few moments alone to collect her thoughts, she struggled with her latest truth. The voice sounded familiar but she couldn't place it. It would nag her, just out of reach, but eventually she would remember.

Sunlight filtered through the blinds and created a basket weave pattern on her comforter. The scent of frying bacon had her stomach grumbling, a nice, normal feeling. She had not been hungry for the last two weeks and had only managed to choke food down to get her strength back. And to keep Brian happy. He hadn't left her side since she was discharged from the hospital except to work. Every day Brian relieved her mom and dad who had dropped everything to be with her while she recuperated. It was amazing to wake up each morning in Brian's arms.

A concussion, broken ribs, a sprained wrist had plagued her. But she needed her life back. Shamus, although willing, could not cover for her forever. Dizzy, she ignored the pounding in her head and sat cautiously on the edge of her bed to get her bearings.

"Good morning, love. Are you OK?" Brian's voice

made her jump. He leaned casually against the door jam, a sexy smile lighting his face. *Oh, he is beautiful and he loves me. Pinch me.*

An old-fashioned bib apron partially covered his bare chest. The apron, included in a gift basket from a local Italian restaurant owner who seemingly forever would repay his debt to Matty for saving his pup's life, hadn't been designed to fit her lover's physique. She read the words printed on the apron out loud, "If you like my pasta, wait 'til you taste my sausage."

Laughing so hard tears streamed down her cheeks, her side hurt like hell as she gasped for breath.

Brian knelt down on the floor in front of her, his hands encasing her face. "It's so good to see you laugh." He kissed her lips, whisper light, a balm for her body and spirit. "Happy Thanksgiving."

"I forgot it was Thanksgiving. I've been living in a fog lately."

"How do you feel?"

"Wonderful." She slid her arms around his neck and untied the apron. It slipped down his granite hard chest followed by her teasing fingers. Matty's stomach constricted with need. Her gentle kiss grew more demanding as she channeled that need, reveled in it. The taste of coffee and bacon on his tongue made her hungrier.

"Oh no, you don't." Brian chuckled and tugged gently to unfasten her arms.

She tightened them instead and leaned backward to draw him into bed with her. "Please. Just lie next to me and hold me." Matty scooted over in the bed and patted the mattress next to her, striking a seductive pose.

Narrowing his eyes, he responded, "OK, but no funny stuff." He grinned and tossed the apron on the floor. Propping two pillows behind his back, he sat leaning against the headboard and enfolded her tenderly in the fortress of his arms. Resting her cheek on his chest, she rubbed small circles over soft chest hair and defined ridges of muscle, inching towards the taut skin under his low-slung jeans. Lowering her head she trailed kisses along his torso up to his neck until her eyes were level with his.

"We can't do this, darling. You've been so sick," he reminded.

She nibbled his bottom lip, eyes wide on his, fully ready to do 'this' and more.

"You promised no funny stuff." His smoldering eyes held hers, his lips passive, hers for the taking.

Her fingers explored down the warm skin of his torso blindly until she encountered the button on his jeans, flicked it open, inched the zipper down.

"Do you think this is funny?" She challenged, her voice husky with desire. Before he could answer she laid her hands on either side of his smooth-shaven face and straddled his hips.

Crisscrossing her arms to grab the hem of her nightgown, she stripped it off over her head. "Don't you want me?"

"I have never wanted anything more in my life." His rough hands caressed her waist, kneaded the small of her back and then pressed her tightly against his chest. "Are you sure?" His warm breath fanned the crown of her head.

"Oh yes, I'm positive."

His hands cupped her bottom and elevated her so she could encompass him with her body, accept and hold him inside, filled completely. His hips rose and fell in gentle, considerate rolls until she matched his rhythm and then took the lead to move harder, faster, skyward. Lost, mindless, consumed, she surrendered to the passion that had been building for weeks.

Matty collapsed against his chest after reaching peaks she had never dreamed possible. For several minutes, she lay semi-sleeping atop him, utterly sated. She raised her head and found him staring at her. The tender gleam in his sea blue eyes brought tears to hers.

His brow knit as his thumb caught a tear at the corner of her eye. "Oh, love, I'm sorry. Did I hurt you?"

"I have never been better in my life. I wish we could stay like this forever."

Brian hugged her against his heart, the beat steady, slow against her breasts.

"If you want to stay like this all day we can. I'll just call Kay and tell her you're not up to a Sullivan Thanksgiving. Or I'll take you over to Shamus' place in your nightgown and you can be comfortable with your family around."

"You really would do that for me, wouldn't you?"

"Anything for you."

A red ball, glistening with dog spit, plopped on the bed against Brian's leg.

"Oops. I think we woke the kid." Brian chuckled. Clyde sat patiently on the floor next to the bed waiting for Brian to toss the ball.

"Hey buddy. It's Thanksgiving. Where's your football?" Clyde bolted away with a skittering barrage of nail clicks growing more distant along the upstairs hall, thudding down the carpeted stairs and then approaching louder and louder on the return trip. The dog appeared with a stuffed football in his mouth. Brian sat on the edge of the bed, reached out a hand, and wrestled it away. He tossed the toy out the door on an angle into the hallway beginning an endless game of fetch, if Clyde had his way.

"I'll take my shower while you guys play." Matty swung her legs over the side of the bed and stood, not the least bit self-conscious now with him.

"Are you sure you are up to going out?

"I want to. I'm sick of being the patient. I feel better than I have in a long time. No more nightmares or anything." She walked between his legs, her breasts brushing soft chest hair and kissed him, a delicious satisfaction that never seemed enough and had to be repeated often. "Thank you for everything."

"My pleasure."

****

Cars dotted the street leading up to Kay and Mike's house. Matty's nervous stomach turned. The egg she had quickly forced down after her shower was upsetting her stomach. Her hands went clammy, slipping on the car door handle as she opened it and stepped out of the car. *The Sullivans are a force to be reckoned with. And now I'm officially Brian's...lover. Hope his family approves.*

A crowd of dazzling, handsome men stood in the driveway tossing a football lazily back and forth.

"Finally Uncle Brian. We thought you'd never get here," Mikey called. Like a new colt, he was all legs and arms. "Let's pick sides. I get Uncle Brian."

"Well, thanks a lot. I would think you would pick your old man first, and where are your manners?" Mike Lynch strode over to the car and hugged Matty.

"I'm sorry. Hello, Miss Connors." A rush of red dotted the adolescent's cheeks.

"How are you, Matty?" Mike assessed her with his physician's clinical eyes. "Let me help you with that." He took the box of candy Matty clutched tightly in her hand.

Brian ran around the front of the car, shoving the case of wine they had brought into Mike Jr.'s arms.

"You're so pale. Do you need to sit down?" His arm encircled her shoulder.

"I'm fine. Sorry. I just got out of the car too quickly. Don't fuss around me. I'm so embarrassed." She waved him off.

"You have nothing to be embarrassed about." Joe hurried over to her take her hand. "You've been through a nightmare."

"Let's get her inside." Patrick shut the passenger door behind her.

Jean Sullivan approached with regal strides down the brick path.

"Lovely to see you again, Matty." Her white hair gleamed in the sunshine. "You men just go ahead and play your game."

Jean crooked her elbow offering an arm to Matty. Placing a light hand over Jean's bicep, Matty accompanied the matriarch along the front walk.

Twisting her head to glimpse over her shoulder, Matty drew courage from Brian's wide smile. Brian hoisted the box of wine out of Mikey's arms and held it near Mike's hand. "Put the candy on top. I'll be right back. Finish picking the sides." He caught up with her in three strides and followed inside the house.

In the den, where apparently all the Sullivan ladies had assembled, Matty chose a seat on a comfortable couch next to Bobbie.

"I'll go join the game?" Brian cocked his head in Matty's direction.

She smiled at him, although tempted to beg him to stay until she had a handle on how or if she'd fit in with the women. "Have fun."

"Boy, Mom, you and Daddy sure made handsome men." Kay laughed.

"Uh huh. They are yummy," Bobbie agreed. Emma curled one hand around the bottle Bobbie held and sucked noisily.

"Yes, Mrs. Sullivan. I couldn't agree more." Jean returned Matty's grin, apparently delighted with her opinion.

Relaxing in the warm company of women, Matty tried unsuccessfully to forget about the morning truth. Although her truths had brought her into this wonderful, loud, crazy family, the new inner suspicion of impending tragedy for them was vehemently unwanted. *Who spoke in a familiar voice? Not Dad or Shamus, thank God. Who was the man in trouble? Dear God, it seems like he's going to die.* She could only hope for another truth that might help prevent sorrow from hitting this welcoming family again.

Bobbie turned animated eyes on her. "Matty, I have been dying to talk to you about your extrasensory gift. I'm fascinated. Joe told me you have never been wrong, including on this case that just closed."

"I have no control over the truths that come to me. Lately I wish they wouldn't come at all." The seemingly dire recent truth a sorrowful echo in her mind, Matty needed to change the subject. *If only I could pick and choose which truths I let in.*

Two little girls clad in identical jeans and Hannah Montana T-shirts scampered into the den. "Aunt Matty. Aunt Matty."

Flattered that Kay's girls remembered her, Matty was touched they referred to her as "aunt Matty" again.

'Did Mommy ask you yet?" queried the girl who wore an *Amanda* gold necklace.

"Ask me what?" *They are adorable, and so far, I can't tell them apart at all, aside from the nametag necklaces.*

"Mommy told us she would ask you about getting a puppy," Amanda explained.

The twins wiggled like puppies themselves.

"Daddy and I said *maybe* we would get a puppy," Kay interrupted.

"Please. Please."

"A puppy is a big responsibility," Matty cautioned.

"We know." Amanda answered, her sky blue eyes open wide.

"We promise to take care of her." Peggy crossed her heart.

"When your mommy and daddy are ready, I promise to help you find the perfect dog."

"Thank you, Aunt Matty," the girls chirped in unison, racing out the door. "Amy! Mary! We're getting a puppy!" they hollered as they pounded up stairs.

"They sure turned that maybe into a yes indeedy." Kay snorted.

"I hope I didn't say anything to encourage that." Matty bit the corner of her lip.

"Hell no. They're connivers." Dimples bloomed in Kay's cheeks reminding Matty of her Brian's smile.

"You might want to think about adopting an older dog. Most of them are house broken. Unfortunately we've had a quite a few dogs abandoned recently. It breaks my heart that people can't afford their pets and are forced to give them up. Poor Shamus. He has six dogs right now. All left on his doorstep. He's such a softie."

"I've read about that in the paper," Molly mentioned, shifting a toddler boy to her other hip. "Danny and I were talking the other night about getting a dog. Maybe we can help your brother out. You look a little pale. How are you feeling?"

"Good really. Happy to be well again and if it's OK with my doctor," she tilted her head at Molly, "I hope to go back to work on Monday."

"You can as long as you don't push yourself and start slowly."

"I promise."

"What are you promising, darling?" Brian, carrying the tangy aroma of outdoor athletics, his shirt drenched with sweat, sat on the arm of the couch and bent down to kiss Matty on the tip of her nose.

"I promised to help Kay when and if she decides to get the girls a dog. And I promised I would take it slow when I go back to work on Monday."

"Monday. Isn't that a little too soon?"

"Molly said it's OK."

"No way that ball crossed the line," Joe contended, stalking with Danny into the room.

"It was way over the line," Mikey argued. "We win. Right, Uncle Brian?"

"Yep. Your least favorite uncles are sore losers." Brian rubbed his hand in circles on Matty's back. "And they're stuck doing the dishes."

"Speaking of dishes, there won't be any if I don't get the dinner on the table." Kay refused the women's offers for help and disappeared, presumably bound for the kitchen.

"Boys, go get washed up and whoever uses the washroom upstairs, bring the little ones with you when you come back down." Jean apparently did not have to tell her sons more than once. They followed her directions immediately with a little more razzing from the winning team.

****

Three tables had been pushed together covered in beige linen, dressed with candles and homemade paper cornucopias with place settings for seventeen. The family quickly took what must be their traditional positions at the table. Matty sat quietly next to Brian and mentally paired the memorized list of names to all the faces.

"Daddy, would you please say grace?" Kay took her seat at the head of the table.

"It would be my pleasure, baby girl." John Sullivan stood at the other end of the table. His white hair glistened under the crystal chandelier.

"Dear Lord, I'd like to take a few minutes to express my gratitude. I'm thankful for my family, for our health and for my nice soft bed that I get to share every night with the love of my life. I'm thankful right now to be surrounded by those whose lives touch me more than they'll ever possibly know. I am thankful that our family continues to grow with new grandchildren and new children."

Brian reached under the table and squeezed Matty's hand.

"Please, heavenly Father, bless this food that you have provided from thy bounty and bless each of us invited here to my daughter's table. Amen."

A chorus of "amens" filled the dining room and then chaos ensued. Plates passed, voices overlapped interlaced with bursts of laughter.

"Bobbie can you pass me a roll?" Patrick called from the far end of the table.

Bobbie picked up a roll and pitched it down the table toward him. Brian snatched it out of the air.

"Interception! Way to go, Uncle Brian!" Mike Jr. grabbed a roll, wrist angled back for the toss.

"Don't even think about it." Kay drilled out.

Pure entertainment.

Soon conversations quieted, silverware scraped against plates, the occasional, "Delicious," or "Everything's so good," remarks the only accompaniment to the enjoyment of the feast. One by one, forks dropped as Sullivans seemingly had their fill.

"Brian, Joe told me that Matty is not the only one who has visions. Is that true? Are you psychic now? Can you give me the lottery numbers for next week?" Patrick chuckled and sat back in his chair.

Brian brushed a hand over her cheek, his marine blue eyes tender. "I received another truth recently that I haven't told Matty about."

Her eyes widening in amazement, Matty searched his face. "Really?"

"Uh huh."

The door chimes sounded.

"Right on time. Excuse me a sec," Kay said as she pushed back from the table.

Brian plucked Matty's left hand off her lap, gazed at the back of it, turned it and planted his lips in her palm. The intimacy inflamed her cheeks and had her toying with a response that would hardly be appropriate in the midst of the Sullivan family.

Blatant desire smoldered in his eyes. And a glint of amusement. "You're not the only one in the truth department Miss *the* Matty Connors. I think I'm getting the hang of it. Want to hear about it?"

"Can't wait," Patrick quipped.

Shuffling and a din of voices. Matty's mouth fell open as her parents, Shamus and Cara trooped into the dining room behind Kay, smiles beaming.

"Hi, sweetie."

"Mom?"

Matty turned toward Brian, mystified.

"Shall I tell everyone about my truth?" Brian asked.

Matty nodded, her eyes riveted on his face, the rest of their families a blur.

Teasing her, he stroked her forearm lightly. "I saw myself in a tuxedo coming through my front door."

Her heart flip-flopped. "Did you now?"

"Yep." He trailed a thumb lazily down the side of her arm. "Thought it was déjà vu the day of Joe's wedding. But that's not how the scene played out. This time I went to the church, waited at the altar with Joe by my side."

She narrowed her eyes and held his. "Interesting."

"Yep. And the bride came down the aisle toward us. A vision, breath taking. You."

Her heart nearly burst with joy. "It's bad luck to see the bride before the wedding day."

Unblinking he asserted, "I figure it's a theoretical truth."

"How so?"

"Doesn't happen unless the lady says yes."

Matty flung her arms around him, buried her head in his shoulder. "Yes!"

The family erupted.

"Whoa!"

"Way to go, Bri!"

"I think I'm going to cry."

"Congratulations, son!"

"Oh boy, a wedding!"

Springing from the chair, Matty grasped both his hands, tears streaming. "I love you, Brian. I can't wait to marry you."

He stood and enfolded her in his arms. Quaking with elation she clung to him.

"I saw one more thing."

Matty raised her head, curious, and looked deeply in his eyes.

"I saw a ring in my pocket."

Matty arched her eyebrows, her heart pounding. "Do you want me to fish for it?"

Brian's grin pierced her heart. "Please do."

Lowering her hand, her eyes fixed on his pocket seam, a vision flashed in Matty's consciousness.

Bonnie and Clyde curled up on the floor beneath the legs of a bassinette, asleep in a pool of sunshine.

About the Author

K. M. Daughters is the writing team of sisters, Pat Casiello and Kathie Clare. Their penname is dedicated to their parents: Kay and Mickey Lynch. Pat is married to Nick Casiello and has three children, Jen, Emilie and Brian. Kathie is married to Tom Clare and has two sons, Tom and Michael. She has one granddaughter, Natalie, a grandson, Michael John new grandbaby is expected in September.

Visit K. M. Daughters www.kmdaughters.com

Thank you for purchasing this Wild Rose Press publication. For other wonderful stories of romance, please visit our on-line bookstore at www.thewildrosepress.com.

For questions or more information contact us at info@thewildrosepress.com.

The Wild Rose Press
www.TheWildRosePress.com